# Lessons from a Nude Man

## DONNA BESEL

A CIP catalogue record for this book is available from
Library and Archives Canada

ISBN 9781926710303

Edited by Harriet Richards.
Designed and typeset by Donald Ward.
Cover art: photograph by Malak Karsh, from the collection of the author.
Cover design by Tania Wolk, Go Giraffe Go.
Set in Minion Pro.
Printed and bound in Canada at Houghton Boston Printers and Lithographers, Saskatoon.

The publishers gratefully acknowledge the assistance of the Saskatchewan Arts Board, The Canada Council for the Arts, and the Cultural Industries Development Fund (Saskatchewan Department of Culture, Youth & Recreation) in the production of this book.

HAGIOS PRESS
Box 33024 Cathedral PO
Regina SK    S4T 7X2
www.hagiospress.com

*For Allison and Brad*

## Acknowledgements

In 2003, *Prairie Fire* published, "Dead Skunk," a second place winner in their annual contest. This unexpected award convinced me that I could send more stories out into the world. To get to this place, I had plenty of help and support.

Thanks go to Gerard Beirne, a writer from County Tipperary, who read my manuscripts and showed me what a writer's life looked like. I also thank Joan Thomas, who read my work and encouraged me to apply for grants. Sage Hill Writing Experience validated me as a writer, and my instructors, Steven Galloway and Denise Chong, inspired me with their wisdom, generosity, and enthusiasm.

*Prairie Fire* published several of my stories and I thank them for their belief in my skills. Most important, they helped me self-identify as a "boreal writer," through their Boreality Project issues.

I am deeply grateful for my friends at Falcon Trails Resort, Barb Hamilton and Craig Christie, who have offered lifelong care during many adventures and troubles. They gave me time to write at their beautiful cabins, hosted writing workshops, and sold my stories to their guests.

I thank the Manitoba Arts Council for various grants and the amazing Artists in the Schools program, where I have shared my love of creative writing with hundreds of students. I thank the Manitoba Writers' Guild and the many friends, writers and readers, who have encouraged my artistic pursuits.

I am give thanks to my large family, who provide abundant material and inspiration. Also, the unexpected death of my husband gave me clarity and seclusion.

Most important of all, I thank my children, Allison and Bradley, who have waited a long time.

# Contents

# Lessons from a Nude Man

I HADN'T SEEN A PENIS IN TEN YEARS.

After my husband "devolved" — as my daughter called it — he stopped having sex. Some men's mid-life crisis involves younger women and Viagra. Not my husband. For two years, he visited a counselor to sort out his demons. But his desire, always somewhat compromised, had completely evaporated. Even if I begged, I never saw his genitals. He wore his boxers to bed and, when we got up in the morning, he did not remove them. Perhaps he took his underwear off to shower, but I couldn't be sure.

So I was especially surprised when a nude man showed up in my parking lot. I run a bed and breakfast in my house out in the country. As the website says, "Swim, fish, and relax on the dock. Visit our secluded, rustic two-storey cedar home on the shores of Lake Washburn." Secluded means ten kilometres from the nearest town. Not much drive-through traffic.

At first, I'd thought it was Roland, who had just hired me to do the census on my side of the lake. His daughter had been training for years to compete in the Winter Olympics (biathlon) so he needed extra cash. I also needed extra cash. When the strange car showed up, I was busy, opening and closing drawers in my kitchen, looking for my cheque book. I thought maybe Roland had gathered it up along with his piles of government forms. I thought maybe he had found it in his truck and did a U-turn on highway 214 so he could bring it back.

At the sound of a vehicle, I looked out the window. The man in the parking lot did not have my cheque book. What he did have, in his hand, was a pair of jeans. He closed the driver's door of his SUV, a Hyundai Santa Fe, and he put them on, as if he had just climbed out of bed. The Hyundai was a rental; I could tell from the license plates.

Still in a brain fog from nearly flunking the census intelligence test, I answered the door. The man wore sandals and the jeans, no shirt. He smiled at me — medium teeth, white and straight. Thick and freshly trimmed hair, light brown. No visible tattoos or pierced bits.

"Hi, I'm Chris. We've talked on the phone."

"Right! On the phone!"

"I'm from Yorkton. I called about visiting."

"Yorkton?"

"Last year. Around this time. My group's interested in a week or longer. We want to try out a new area. I was in Winnipeg on business so I thought I'd come check out your setup." He waved his arm to encompass my five-bedroom house, with its wide lawn, dock and beach, gazebo, large parking lot. "What a great place!"

He dropped his arm and smiled even broader.

I stared at his shoulders — well-muscled but narrower than mine. Just like my husband. I could see tiny acne scars across his upper torso, barely noticeable under the golden-brown tan.

"Can I come in and look at the rooms?"

"Right! From Yorkton!"

It finally clicked. I had spoken to him several times.

In my aforementioned ad on the bed and breakfast website, the tag-line "alternatives welcome" — intended to solicit gays, artists, organic food-eaters, pagans — had caught his attention.

On the phone, I'd told Chris that my home used to be quiet and private. Until Danny, a hockey player in his late twenties, bought the adjacent log cabin, built in the early fifties and situated on the wide waterfront lot next to my place. The first weekend Danny set up house in the rundown bungalow, he hosted a hundred-car, drunken blow-out in celebration of his beloved team's regional championship. Danny purchased the rotting cabin from a retired farmer who drove out once a week, cut the grass, threw in a fishing line, and drove off before he caught anything. Now pickups, four-wheelers, snowmobiles, motorcycles, and dirt-bikes roared in and out 24/7.

On the phone, I also told Chris it probably wouldn't work.

I didn't tell him how much my reputation was already compromised.

To SUPPLEMENT MY WIDOW'S PENSION, I started operating the bed and breakfast. This was another result of my husband's "devolution." I used to work for him, in his home-based law practice. Now I rent out his former office. I cleared it out and put in a queen-sized bed and two sets of bunks, creating enough sleeping spaces for a family of six. Most nights, I sleep in there, because the queen-sized bed has the firmest mattress in the house. But I don't keep any clothes in that room. I can change sheets and vacate in five minutes.

Our master bedroom is now my office. It's where I write — on the last vestiges of the law office's furniture — an underpowered computer and an over-sized desk. I have plenty of material. Nonfiction and fiction — both equally unbelievable. When B&B guests occupy the queen-sized bed, I sleep on a narrow cot in the corner of my writing room.

"Come in, Chris."

I thought, *What am I doing? He could be a sex fiend.*

Then: *that might not be so bad.*

Chris stepped into the foyer. He smiled again. "Your home is very inviting."

I showed him the three other bedrooms on the lower level, the television room, and the shared washroom and shower. These bedrooms were much smaller, with single beds, intended for individual guests. He said they looked clean and comfortable.

"The kitchen and dining table are upstairs. Where we eat."

I still felt stunned. I was repeating myself and stating the obvious. Or maybe it wasn't so obvious. Our home is built up-side-down. I designed it to accommodate the main floor law office, so clients wouldn't traipse through *our* private lives to spill details about *their* private lives. Long ago, I learned that nobody visits a lawyer unless they have experienced upheaval. Sometimes, the change is for the better, but it usually involves dispute or loss. So our living area was up on the second level. On most days, it felt like we lived in a tree house. When the kids were small, the second-storey view allowed me to keep track of them.

Once we finished the mini-tour, Chris told me again how much he liked the house. Then, in the kitchen, he paused and looked at me.

"Can I take off my pants? So you can get a sense of it. . . . "

*Why not? I did say alternatives.*

I nodded. "Go ahead. I often jump off the dock, with no suit. And I've been in a nude sauna."

I didn't realize this would be different. When I go skinny-dipping, I'm alone, or with women friends. When I went into that clothing optional sauna at the cross-country ski resort in Minnesota, I took off my glasses so they didn't fog up and scorch my nose. I couldn't tell if the pink shapes with dark patches were male or female — especially after a few beers or when the men sat down and tucked in their genitals. Also, I quickly learned it's not polite to lean forward and stare — even if you are nearsighted.

Chris shucked off his jeans and launched into an explanation of naturist philosophy. He told me that naturists believe that all bodies are equal and natural, and there is nothing shocking or immoral about nudity. He expounded on naturist theories and how they helped people accept and celebrate their own bodies, and learn respect for others. He explained that they liked to visit new places, usually with groups of friends. He listed the physical activities they pursued and vacation spots they enjoyed.

While he talked, I nodded and asked occasional questions such as, "How do you handle strangers? Or cops?" and "Where and when is it safe?" and "Is non-sexual nudity possible?"

He answered in full and careful sentences, like a teacher instructing a junior high class on the wonders of reproduction.

I could not wrangle the stampede of random thoughts.

*I'm tired of being embarrassed. He's fit but not stunning. It's flaccid right now but not remarkable — nice to see that male nudists aren't all about their pecs and big packages. This is what real people look like.*

After a couple more questions, he went off on another tangent — more explanations about health and censorship and self-esteem.

*Evangelical — like a Jehovah's Witness — totally convinced of his choices.*

*I've forgotten what a penis looks like. I must remember to keep looking at his face. His eyes. Light and wintry blue. Intelligent. Kind. Is he married?*

Then he told me that his closest friends shared the lifestyle. And his wife and three children, as well as their boyfriends and girlfriends

*Damn, why is he leaning his ass on my kitchen counter? I thought they put towels under their bums when they sit down. He's not cute at all. I wouldn't let my dog do that.*

His next two questions halted my racing thoughts.

"What about the rest of your family? How would they react?"

I inhaled. "Well, I'm a widow. My daughter's at university. There's only me and my son, Tyler."

"How old?"

"Eighteen. He's in his last year of high school."

"Is he interested in nudity?"

"Very much. But I've told him hundreds of times. Real women don't look like that. Porn is made-up garbage. Exploitation."

"Nudism helps. After a short time, people get comfortable.

Are you more relaxed now?"

"Yes, it's like we're just talking." This was a lie. He explained more naturist theories, such as how it teaches their kids not to feel shame and disgust about their own growing bodies and other people's bodies. He told me how commercial media surround and overwhelm us with unrealistic images of air-brushed and ultra-skinny models. How it makes everyone feel they can never measure up. How nudism helps people to be more honest and tolerant and open.

I could not stop checking out his penis. Determined not to stare, I looked over his shoulder at the kitchen clock.

"Oh, shit! I forgot. I have an appointment for an oil change."

"No problem. I'll follow you to the garage and pick you up. You can show me around. I've looked at the web sites for this area. I'd like to check out the hiking trails in the Wolf River Park."

I could not think of one reason why not. He had said, several times, that his "group" included eight people, eager to find a nudist-friendly resort. And he could already envision them sun tanning on my dock. I needed the money. I thought about my visit to the nude sauna and told myself it could work. My son would be at school during the day.

We went outside to our respective vehicles. I looked back. Chris had not put on his pants.

*I hope Danny isn't drinking beer on his back step.*

I raced to the garage. Threw the keys at the mechanic. True to his word, Chris drove into the parking area. I walked over to his Hyundai and opened the door. Still no pants.

My eyebrows must have given me away.

"I drive nude as often as possible."

"Do semi-trailer drivers look down on you?" I giggled at the unintended pun. I assumed truck jockeys could easily peer down into his seat from their higher-up perch.

"We keep clothing handy. For when they pass us. Or we pass them. "

"Oh." I imagined him sliding a towel across his lap.

Then I realized that Greg, the mechanic, had followed me. He wanted to confirm the exact part he planned to order for my Ford Focus. I hopped out and stood in his way so he could not see into the Hyundai. Greg might wonder why I was riding around with a shirtless man, but it *was* especially hot today.

When I got back into the SUV, Chris asked, "Are you still nervous?"

"Yes, I can imagine Greg telling the whole town that a naked stranger picked me up."

"He didn't see a thing. Let's go to the park now. I want to see how open the trails are."

*Maybe it's like people who have sex in exposed places. They want to be discovered.*

When we got to the provincial park, two couples were walking their dogs along the trail that led to the dam and the rapids. The man in the younger pair tugged on a panting black Lab and the older couple strolled behind a gimpy Boston terrier. Chris got out and put on his pants. He stood beside the Hyundai, by the driver's door, similar to the way I first saw him. He explained how naturists often walk without clothing on isolated hiking trails in provincial and national parks. When they hear people approaching, they pull on a pair of shorts and a tee-shirt. Or, if the people look amenable, they will ask permission to pass them by without clothes. We hiked around the picnic site for an hour.

*It feels good to be with a man my age. He's not bad-looking — much cuter than I first thought. Such an appealing smile. So easy to talk to.*

"Let's go behind the dam. I want these jeans off."

*Christ, it's a fucking obsession.*

We walked to the rear of the dam.

"What do you do in the winter time? Yorkton can't be all that warm."

"That's why we want to get out to the country. Especially in the summer. To places like yours. Also, there's a nudist colony twenty kilometres from here and a nude beach on Lake Tamarack."

A tall man with a large-lens camera strolled along the walkway on the top of the dam. Chris kept his pants on while we walked around to the footbridge which led to the Hyundai.

BACK AT THE HOUSE, he asked, "Can I come inside?"

"Sure, we'll get something to drink."

As he followed me up the sidewalk, I put my head down, chuckled into my chest. *Does that sound like a come-on? And how would I explain a nude drunk to Tyler?*

As soon as we got upstairs, Chris doffed his pants and sat down at the table. After he slugged back a glass of water, he said, "I think you have the right attitude. We'd love to stay here."

"What about the all-night parties and nonstop traffic?"

"We can work around him. If he's such a free spirit, maybe he'd like to join us."

*Or maybe Danny's a redneck thug who might view any penis, outside of a shower in a hockey locker room, as a fag alert and therefore fair game. He might pound you like mashed potatoes.*

"Nope. Doesn't seem too open-minded to me."

As I glanced at the well-defined chest across the table, I felt a trickle of sweat slide between my breasts. I took a long sip of water. After the hike, odours wafted up from my crotch and armpits — pungent, stronger than usual. *Can he smell me? Do nudists notice this, or even care?*

"Not like you." He smiled and poured himself another full glass and took another long drink. "But we need to know one thing before I go."

I was glad to hear he planned to leave. His presence exhausted me. I couldn't decide if I wanted to laugh out loud for several minutes or yell at him to leave.

"Would you like to try?"

"What?"

"Take off your clothes?"

I lifted my hand to my tee-shirt. In theory, I admired his defiance of society's taboos. I had been nude in mixed company. Now I could apply my open-minded hypotheses.

I stared at his nipples, at the dark hairs scattered across his chest. He pushed his glass to the side and stood up and walked around the table. Spread his arms wide, as if inviting me to waltz.

I got up and looked into his pale blue eyes, the colour of young flax. He smiled again.

We stood like this for about twenty seconds.

"I can't."

"You looked ready."

"In my head, yes. In my body, no."

"After a couple of minutes, you'd relax."

Globs of moisture pooled on the rims of my eyelids. Hot and tacky, like melted wax. I wanted to cry but the tears stuck.

"I'm a widow. It's been too long. I can't do it."

He nodded and bent to grab his jeans off the back of another chair.

It felt like someone had sliced me open. *How did this strange intimacy develop? I don't know this guy, but I want to lay him down on my expensive mattress and explain. About my life. About the years of frustration. About my husband's sudden twist from mild depression into porn-addicted, full-blown crazy. And then the suicide.*

*And how that self-murder hit like a comet — with its long tail of blame, loss, fear. How the rumours leaked out like gasoline on water, spread by a posse of spiteful in-laws, who all lived within a hundred-kilometre radius. They set that gas on fire — accused me of being a money-grubber. A lethal lesbian. A bad mother. A terrible cook who couldn't boil water. Whatever.*

*After the suicide, they wanted me to move to another prov-*

ince, as quickly as possible. They wanted me to vacate my be-loved home, leave behind my long-time friends, and forget the community where I had lived for more than thirty years. I don't know why but they believed if I disappeared, people would stop talking.

Chris did not seem upset by my rejection. "I understand. I've tried a few places. Not everyone is comfortable with the idea. I really enjoyed our time together. Thanks for the tour. Maybe we'll find another resort."

I swallowed the hard knot in my throat. "A friend of mine rents out a place on an isolated lake. They call it their "eco-cab-in." Composting toilet, solar panels, gravity-fed shower, wood heat. Maybe your group would. . . . "

"Sounds great, can you give me the details?"

And then he left.


I CRIED FOR HALF AN HOUR. When Tyler came home, I dried my puffy eyes and stopped.

I told him and he laughed at me. "You should have agreed. I lo-o-o-ve naked women."

"Yeah, I know." I felt a stab of panic under my breasts, right along the bra line. *Hadn't I warned him that women are not objects? Hadn't I told him porn messed up real-life relationships?*

For a week after the nude visit, I felt tired and sad. Dis-appointed in myself — like I had missed a cruise ship or a much-anticipated vacation — one that might have changed my life. I had been shown a different way to view my body, but I didn't have the courage to cast off the shackles of my jeans and tee-shirt and underwear.

And I still haven't seen another penis.

# Fare Well

GINA'S MOTHER LAY IN THE OAK COFFIN, COCOONED IN SATIN pillows.

Her dark hair was pinned back and she was dressed in a white blouse and navy wool suit. Her cheeks glowed like marble, bloodless and cool. Caked with makeup, her features had been rendered smooth and ageless, a wax caricature of Gina's real mother.

The casket and its brass fittings gleamed under stained-glass light fixtures set in the vaulted ceiling. Although it was a drab winter afternoon, a soft yellow light filled the corners of the room, making every surface appear as if it had been illuminated by a waning fire.

Gina stared at her mother's forehead, cheekbones, hair for a full minute, but could not detect any evidence of the final indignities. Seeing her mother there, surrounded by plush fabrics, made up like a movie star, dressed in the clothes she wore to play the church organ, caused a slow bile to burn up the girl's throat. She held her mother's hand for a few seconds and then lifted her fingers to her nose. The embalming fluid had overwhelmed the all-too-familiar scent of bleach and laundry detergent. Gina touched her mother's cheek once and turned away.

*Déja vu,* she thought. But that made no sense. In all the fourteen years of her life, she had never been to a funeral.

The brick funeral home was located in the middle of downtown Winnipeg. Gina wanted to run from that muffled room, escape those oak-paneled walls. But she had lived in the bush all her life and had no idea where to go. She stumbled away from the casket, over to the family pew, and sat next to her youngest sister, and her seven other siblings. Through a glass block barrier which separated them from the larger sanctuary, she watched dark silhouettes file into the chapel.

THE LAST DAY SHE SAW HER MOTHER ALIVE was two weeks earlier, on the second Sunday in December. The wind had died down during the night, but the temperatures had hovered near minus twenty and the dry snow squeaked underfoot. Gina made porridge for breakfast and fed the younger kids. After she cleaned up the dishes, she decided it was warm enough for a ride.

Every morning, she turned out their four saddle horses, cleaned stalls, and threw a couple of timothy bales in the outdoor manger. Her young mare hadn't been ridden all week, except for short daily trips for a drink. Because their stable had no running water, every night after supper Gina rode her mare and herded the three other horses down the hill to nearby Black Lake. Sometimes she persuaded one or two of the other kids to help her. Gina always carried an axe to chop a hole in the ice. Some days it took over an hour, depending on the thickness.

In the dim hallway between the three adjoining bedrooms, Gina rummaged around in a box of spare clothes for long underwear. Jeans, shirts, towels, and sheets spilled onto the floor from a laundry basket. She plucked up bundles of sweat-stinky clothes and stuffed them back into the basket. Several other boxes and baskets, filled to the brim, lined the narrow entrance to the bedrooms.

Her mother called out from her bedroom at the end of the hall. "The kids don't have anything clean for school. You know it takes two days to dry clothes."

For a moment, her mother sounded almost normal, fretting and pissed off about the never-ending piles of laundry. But the angry tone quickly faded, choked down by fatigue and sadness.

Despite Gina's eagerness to get outside, she could not ignore the laundry or the despair in her mother's voice. She entered her parents' room and looked at the crumpled bed. Her mother had been curled up in it for the past three days — like a fox in its den, in a fetal half-circle, hidden in a nest of sheets. The room stunk like dirty socks, sawdust, perspiration, perfume.

Her mother pushed strands of hair away from her red-rimmed eyes and struggled to raise herself. She couldn't get much higher than the pillows. Her skin resembled fireplace ashes, gray and thin and brittle.

Gina glanced back through the open door at the piles of dirty clothing. *Shit. Must be at least five or six loads. I'll have to hang them outside. They'll freeze solid and then I'll have to haul them back inside to thaw out and dry. Should take me all day.*

Her mother sighed, wiped her eyes, and ran her palms down her cheeks. "Where's Mary? Can't she help?"

Gina wanted to spit but swallowed the phlegm. "She's gone to Marc's. You know, that half-wit RCMP she likes to mate."

Her mother sighed again and asked for a glass of water.

Gina turned toward the kitchen, her cheeks burning with a furious pity. Her mother hadn't eaten any breakfast and probably no one had asked if she needed help to go the bathroom. Hours ago, Gina's father had headed for the bush. Her two older brothers, who cut and hauled logs with him, never asked her if she needed anything. Several times, Gina had seen them giggling into their fists when their father called their mother a lazy bitch.

A COUPLE OF MONTHS EARLIER, Gina's father had taken his wife to see Doctor Campbell in Strachan. She visited him often, but he never questioned the recurring fractures and black eyes. Doctor Campbell wore wrinkled dark suits and striped ties, and looked chubby and pale from too much sitting. After the examination, he declared her to be trapped in a bad menopause, caused by eight pregnancies, three miscarriages, and twenty years of overwork. He prescribed tranquilizers and told her to take it easy. Get the kids to do more.

By November, their mother started to fall down — almost every day. When she collapsed, the kids dragged her to bed. Sometimes she stayed there. Sometimes she got up and made supper. Their father took her back to the pudgy doctor and asked him to fix her so she could make meals and do laundry. Instead, Doctor Campbell committed her to a psych ward.

She stayed for a couple of weeks, during the same time as Gina's best friend's mother, Darlene, who was also menopausal. A year earlier, Darlene's husband had died of a heart attack. In the following months, she was diagnosed with a "nervous breakdown" and had endured a series of shock treatments.

Darlene told Gina how the nurses forced her mother to get up out of bed and walk. Even when Gina's mother fell down, they kept prodding her. Darlene wasn't too clear on the ugly details, but Gina decided that her mother must have been given shock treatments, too. No adult ever told Gina or the rest of the kids the exact diagnosis.

GINA BROUGHT HER MOTHER a glass of water and two slices of toast covered with peanut butter and raspberry jam. She put the glass and plate on the side table, pulled her mother upright in the bed, and handed her the food.

Her mother chewed on the toast for several minutes. She put down the plate, picked up the glass, took a long sip, and asked, "Can you do the clothes?"

The effort of sitting up, eating, and speaking seemed to have exhausted her, squeezed out the last of her remaining energy. She closed her eyes and waited.

Gina glanced at the baskets in the hallway and grimaced at the injustice of it all.

"I want to ride my horse."

"I don't get to do what I want."

Gina rolled her eyes. "I'm not the mother. You are."

Her mother started to answer but stopped. She buried her face in the sheets. Gina could tell by the heaving motions she was crying. Her head bobbed into the thin material — silent, but violent movements, like a swimmer breast-stroking into the waves. Gina felt like a shit for reminding her mother she couldn't do her job.

Gina grabbed the crumb-filled plate and empty glass, marched out of the room and booted the row of laundry baskets. They spilled. A sour part inside her felt good about kicking dirty clothes all over the hallway. She headed for the dingy kitchen and threw the plate and glass into the sink.

Two hours later, Gina had washed and pegged four loads of laundry onto the sagging line behind the house. As she finished up the last basket, a five-point buck approached the compost pile. He dipped his head and nuzzled deep into the pile, rooting for potato and carrot peels. Gina stopped and walked closer. She picked up a browned apple slice and offered it to him. He sniffed and chomped hard — so hard the apple chunk slid from her numb fingers. Gina leaned over to retrieve it. The buck, irritated by her interference, reared up and stomped both of his sharp front hooves into the back of her head. The impact knocked her face first into the compost. Rotten vegetables and egg shells jammed into her mouth. She spit them out and yelped.

The buck spun away, back into the pine forest.

Inside the house, Gina washed her scraped cheeks, fingered the lumps on the back of her head, and stared at the grainy bathroom mirror. Tears stung her eyes as she thought about the unfairness of washing other people's dirty laundry, and the unfairness of being booted face-down into half-frozen compost. By a stupid deer.

She dried her hands and heard muffled crying and moans.

The bathroom, about the size of two kitchen tables, was attached to the left side of the entrance porch. In the porch, a twelve-by-twelve room, washing machine, tubs, closets, shelves, barrel stove, and a cement cistern were crowded together. Both bathroom and porch had been added after the main house was built. To allow heat from the barrel stove to flow into the bedrooms, a rectangular hole had been cut into her parents' room and fitted with an iron grate.

The sounds came from this grate, near the ceiling. Gina wanted to stuff a blanket into it, but couldn't figure out how to do this without setting fire to the house. The nearby stovepipe glowed from the four-foot logs she had just rammed into the barrel stove. She did this chore automatically, without thinking. In such freezing weather, the house cooled quickly if no one refilled the stove.

Gina had heard her mother's sobs many times before. So she hardened her heart and grabbed her barn-smelling coveralls. Shadows from the pails and tubs stacked on top of the cistern reminded her that the laundry chores had chewed up the warmest hours. If she wanted to ride in daylight, she needed to hurry.

She flung open the back door and raced across the snow-packed yard. She had forgotten to let out the horses.

Her mare liked her morning feed; she might try to buck Gina off and head back to the barn. So she hardened her heart again and decided to risk it. She bridled the mare and led her outside. Then she chased the three other horses out the barn door and pitched them a few forks full of hay.

The mare tried to dump Gina — twice — as she rode through the pine forest behind the house. Because of the cold, she rode bareback so it took some fancy clinging to stay upright. After an hour, the mare had tired enough to give up trying to pitch Gina off and plodded along, head hanging low, shoulders and neck whitened by crystals of frozen sweat. Horse and rider returned, without further excitement, to the silent barn.

By THE TIME GINA ENTERED THE BACK PORCH and peeled off her coveralls, the metal stove had stopped pinging and the stovepipe had stopped glowing. The floors in the house felt stiff and cold. She could hear CBC on the television set in the living room, but it appeared that no one watching it was old enough or strong enough to throw more logs into the stove. Gina loaded it again and went to check on her mother. She hadn't moved. But she was no longer crying.

Gina started peeling potatoes.

After about half an hour, her two older brothers and father returned. Tired and chilled from their day in the bush, they wanted food, and lots of it. They devoured moose stew and mashed potatoes, and left the kitchen. Her father went into the far bedroom to nap and her brothers went into the living room to watch CBC with the younger kids. Everyone assumed that she would clean up the kitchen, even though she still had to water the horses and bed them down for the night. No one else wanted to go outside. The temperature had dropped below minus twenty-five.

When she got back from the lake, she brushed the rim of frost from her scarf and hood, and removed stiff layers of barn clothes. Through the grate above the stove, she could hear her two older brothers laughing.

"She hasn't got out of bed all day," their father said.

"It's Sunday. She wants a day off." Michael, two years older than Gina, said this quietly, as if unsure if he should agree with their father.

A chair slammed against the wall. "Nope, she's faking. *And* she's a lazy bitch!"

The oldest brother, Brent, taller and broader than his father, drove the pulp truck and worked as hard as a grown man. He said, "Maybe it's time to go back to the doctor. I could take her into town tomorrow morning."

Their father snorted. "And get her to buy some goddamned Christmas presents. She's been lying in that bed for weeks.

Who's had time to worry about gifts for all you kids?"

Gina heard the sound of sheets being yanked.

"Look at that! She's pissed herself. Mike, get your sister."

As Gina hung up the last of her outdoor clothes, Mike came into the porch and gestured for her to follow him.

"I heard what you said. More laundry for me."

When they went into their parents' room, their father had already cleared the blankets off the bed. Their mother sat on the edge of the bare mattress, shivering and mumbling.

"That's it. Get her ready. We're going to the hospital. Let that idiot doctor worry about stinking wet sheets."

He grabbed the bundle of bedding. Then he looked at Gina and her two brothers, yelled, "Fuckin' lazy bitch!" and stomped out of the room. Brent followed.

Gina pulled clothes out of drawers and closets, and she and Mike started dressing their mother. It was to be their last physical contact with her.

Mike frowned and said, "I never had to dress a woman before. It doesn't seem right for a guy to be doing this."

To Gina, it seemed beyond funny.

As they stripped off the damp nightgown, she laughed. As she cupped breasts into a bra and Mike fastened it at the back, she laughed. As they hoisted up underpants, zipped up wool slacks and pulled on a thick sweater their mother had knitted, she laughed. As she knelt by the two cold feet and rolled up the socks, she laughed.

When she sent Mike to fetch their mother's winter coat and boots, she cried.

Her mother looked at Gina for half a minute, but her eyes could not focus. Gina grabbed her mother's right hand and, for one minute, held it with a crushing grip. Gina stopped crying; her mother's whole body kept shaking, even though she was now dry and fully clothed.

Gina heard the old station wagon rumbling outside the window so she sent Mike to tell their father they had finished dressing her. When Mike came back into the bedroom, huffing from the cold, they wrapped her arms over their shoulders and lifted her up. With one kid jammed under each armpit, they walked her out to the Chevy.

Then they sat at home and waited.

Doctor Campbell, their regular family physician, had already left for his annual winter vacation in Florida.

The day after the hospital admitted their mother, a young surgeon ordered some x-rays. They found the tumour, but it was too large and too tangled into her brain to operate.

A week before Christmas, their mother died.

So Gina saw her mother's face one last time, at her funeral, three days before Boxing Day. And saw that the woman in the coffin did not resemble the woman they had carried out to the car.

# Hawksley Workman
# and the Worst Motel in Canada

"Did somebody say we'll be home for dinner on time?"
— Hawksley Workman, "Sad House Daddy"

We left Port Perry, Ontario, on the Sunday after my nephew's wedding.

Jason, handsome doctor, had married Shayla, cute physiotherapist, on a dilapidated island estate. The weekend had included: large tent, July heat, sushi appetizers, towering elms, classical quartet, gourmet meal, chocolate fountain, and scenic lake quietly lapping behind the heartfelt ceremony.

That morning, the hung-over wedding party and various relatives from out-of-town had devoured stacks of blueberry pancakes, piled up chairs, took down the tent, picked up garbage, removed Chinese lanterns from trees, drank beer and played with my nephew's golden retriever, Heidi.

Around eleven-thirty, in a fog of alcohol excess and sleep deprivation, we pulled out of the parking lot, stuffed with breakfast and delusions of a close-knit family. Although my youngest nephew chose to smoke up behind the log barn and didn't show his face, the drawn-out leave-taking did not mar our happiness. I maneuvered my 2005 Ford Focus back across the narrow causeway.

My son Josh, sitting beside me, pulled out our frayed map of Ontario. He said, "Let's explore. Take a different route."

Too busy dodging holes on the single track leading to the

mainland, I didn't respond.

My twenty-year-old daughter, Hanna, moaned loudly from the rear seat. She had already pushed two pillows into the corner, preparing for a nap. Six years older than Josh, she had little patience for his whims and naïveté. During the past fourteen years, at least once a month, she told him how much she regretted that she was not an only child.

She said, "I have to be at work on Tuesday. We can't piss around on the way home."

I glanced at Josh and at the map, and pointed. "It's all Canadian Shield. Tourist country. We should be able to find a motel."

After fifteen minutes of heated discussions and jarring ruts, we decided to head through the Lake Simcoe region and stay as close as possible to Lake Superior's northern shores. On the drive down to the wedding, we'd taken the longer loop, through the remote mining and logging towns of Beardmore, Geraldton, Longlac, Kapuskasing, Cochrane, Iroquois Falls, Kirkland Lake, and North Bay. Whizzing along in our tiny car, I'd imagined far-flung lakes, interspersed with granite outcrops and billions of trees, stretching to the tundra. Although we had only stopped for gas refills, meals, two sleeps in our tent, and numerous photos of giant statues, it took almost twenty-four hours of driving to get to Port Perry. I did not want to do it again.

Josh poked at the map and read off the towns north of the island in his best Monty Python "upper class twit" accent — a variation of the Queen's English. "East Gwillimbury, Uxbridge, Gravenhurst, Bracebridge, Huntsville."

Hanna yelped. "Huntsville! Hawksley Workman's home town! Maybe he'll be hanging around. He records in an old schoolhouse there."

In her sweet, sad, soprano, she sang the song Hawksley had recorded with his brother. "*This summer I'm gonna get us a motor bike, to ride up to Ilfracombe and over to Ravenscliffe.*"

While she rambled through the chorus and all the verses, we bumped onto the main highway.

Josh ran his fingers across the map. "Hey, those are real places."

All three of us love Hawksley's music. His songs, filled with quirky lyrics and soulful humour, captivated us. He could howl and moan and whisper, spilling his fierce confidences, creating urgent intimacies, and never miss a note. We marveled at his musical genius and his wild leaps between moods and instruments when he played live. And oh — how we loved his concerts — full of glam rock bravado, cabaret posturing, and unfettered joy at making music.

On the drive from Manitoba, we had listened to every one of his CDs. Each time we played his ballad, "Sweet Hallelujah," Josh asked for a repeat. We didn't mind; we had played this song when we buried their father's ashes. It made us cry, but we agreed we liked the ache of it. Right now we had reasons to smile, excited by our proximity to Hawkley's stomping grounds. We headed north, light-hearted and full-bellied.

By noon, we arrived at Wasaga Beach. Near the crowded boardwalk, we met up with friends who had sold their Lake Winnipeg cottage, near Gimli, four years ago. We hadn't seen them since they moved to Burlington. Although we had wanted to visit before the wedding, I dreaded facing Highway 401 traffic in our overloaded and undersized car, so we arranged to meet post-nuptials.

The afternoon of hot sun and white sand added to our euphoria. After a trip to the concession for chili burgers and soggy fries, we lingered on the beach. My children built sand castles and buried my friends' kids, up to their necks. By the time we returned to the parking lot, it was seven o'clock. Stinking from sunscreen and wet towels, we kissed and hugged and promised to visit.

Along the edge of Georgian Bay, our Focus slipped past hundreds of grand summer homes. Josh read the names again, without the fake accent. "Woodland, Deanlea, Bluewater, Wendake, Wymbolwood, Ossossane, Balm, Cawaja, Wahnek-ewaning."

We turned away from the bay cottages and argued for a few minutes about going to Huntsville. I slipped Hawksley's "Lovers/ Fighters" in the CD player and headed north, hoping to stay near the lake for as long as possible.

My happiness deflated as the kilometres slid by. In its place, I began to dread the half-continent of boreal forest that lay ahead. Near Crooked Bay, I asked Hanna to drive. "Look, I know you don't like strange roads, but there's not much traffic. You can do it."

After three-quarters of an hour behind the wheel, she pulled over. I had slept off a portion of my hangover, so I switched places. Rocks and trees and lakes continued to flow past the windows.

A mottled orange blob with its left edge chewed off rose in the twilight. I changed the CD. Next pick — Hawksley's "Almost a Full Moon."

I said, "I know this CD is kind of Christmas-y but it fits. Look at that beautiful moon. 'Waxing gibbous,' I believe it's called."

Josh yawned, pulled out his ear buds and looked up from his iPod. "Are we near Huntsville?"

"Not yet."

He picked up the map. After a few minutes, he said, "I think we've taken the wrong road."

Hanna was asleep. I tried to read the map that Josh held near my shoulder, but the Focus started to wander. Some asshole driving an eighteen-wheeler, his massive grill almost scraping my rear bumper, blared his horn at me. My tiny car shuddered as he swooped past in an air-sucking vortex of dazzling chrome and manic mud flaps. The drop-off on the side of the road startled me. We were not in corn-growing farmland any more.

I turned off highway 69 and drove northwest, hoping to get closer to Huntsville, and changed the CD to "For Him and the Girls."

"Sweet Hallelujah" — the one we played at the cemetery, came on again.

I opened and closed my eyes several times to clear the wetness. The memory of the grave-side scene always gave me a lump in my throat. I pictured digging through Manitoba gumbo, my children taking turns with the shovel. I pictured Jason and Shayla, the newlyweds. Since my husband's death, I found weddings intolerable. I succumbed to the music and the sorrow, and drove into the gathering dusk, with a few tears sliding down my cheeks.

The scenery had changed to rough, swampy areas alternating with rough, rocky areas, much different from the "Group of Seven" topography I expected. Resort cabins and motels popped up amongst sparse towns and frequent lakes, but they looked deserted, rundown — Tom Thompson's nightmares, perhaps.

Next song — "Sad House Daddies."

Hawksley crooned, "*Sad house daddy, open up the door. We're all good people; we're all good people down here.*" He sang this mournful line again and again. The soft, breathy vocals suited my mood and the dark landscape.

I coughed and Josh roused himself.

He said, "I'm hungry. Have we found a place to stay?"

"Not yet. I expected more motels. We'll try the next one."

Fifteen minutes passed. I saw a row of cabins on the outskirts of a small town. The Lilac Resort. I got out and walked to the cabin with the blinking "Office" sign, but did not spot any lilacs. Just chipped gray sidewalks and chipped purple doors. The wide man at the desk smiled and told me they had no vacancy.

I returned to the Focus. "Who holds a catch-and-release fishing derby on Sunday?"

"Maybe they're all too drunk to go home," Josh said.

I drove for another half hour and found Lakeside Inn. By now, the moon had climbed higher. I approached the office, serenaded by a chorus of frogs. Someone had boarded up the door. That explained the weeds in the parking lot. It couldn't have been too long ago. The plywood on the windows still looked yellow, not fuzzed-up gray. And lights still flashed in the big overhead sign.

Back on the highway, it dawned on me.

At one time, resorts in this part of Ontario might have catered to weekend anglers and families who liked dinky cabins or trailer villages. But these tourists had disappeared. The new ones wanted hot tubs, hot showers, hot bars, water slides, and zip lines.

Hanna woke up. "Are you going to drive all night?"

"No, I'd like to find a cheap motel. We've tried a couple of places."

She sighed, flipped through her CD case, pulled out a disc and passed it to Josh. "Here, play this one. It's "(Last Night We Were) the Delicious Wolves.""

I said, "We're not anywhere near Huntsville. We might have found something there. It's a larger town. Not like these emptied-out villages. It's hard to tell how big they are from looking at the map. They have names, but no population."

"I'm hungry," said Josh.

"Sorry, no twenty-four hour gas stations. It's like no one travels this road, night or day."

"Except big-ass trucks." Hanna shifted in the rear seat; her knees dug into my back. "So what are we going to do?"

"We'll stop at the next place with a vacancy sign."

Twenty minutes later, my head started to droop. I shook it and slapped my cheek. When I opened the window up a narrow crack to feel the night air, I smelled the familiar muskeg and balsam. The road elevations had changed. Long curves of a shimmering asphalt river undulated before my eyes. I took this as a positive sign; more scenic country meant more tourists, which meant more accommodations. It also meant the night driving was more dangerous. I was half asleep.

After another double S-bend, I spotted a long, low building near the highway, perched on a slight rise. Despite the forest shadows, the motel's stucco walls glowed in the moonlight. A backlit yellow sign said "Hideaway Motel." I slowed to twenty and pulled onto the rutted gravel.

The grass on the front lawn looked strangely tall for mid-July, almost ready to be cut and baled. Fluorescent fixtures mounted under the roof's overhang reflected off dark windows and doors. I counted six rooms on each wing. Toward the centre of the building, in the largest window, red neon flashed "VACANCY."

I sang along with Hawksley to wake up my passengers, and stopped in front of the central room where a lop-sided "Office" sign hung over a door. Like the parking lot in the previous place, weeds grew through cracks. I was too exhausted to care. I rang a doorbell and heard dogs barking inside the office. After five minutes and three more jabs at the doorbell, I swore and walked back to the Focus.

"What happened?" Hanna stood behind the car's trunk, in hopes that I had come to tell them I had keys and she could unload.

"Nobody answered." I yawned. "Maybe we'll have to sleep in the car."

Josh had opened the rear window and now looked at me in a stupor, blinking, his blond hair a tangled mess and his face pale blue under the fluorescent lights. He pointed to a spot behind me.

"Did you want a room?" It was a soft voice, barely audible over the rattling chorus of the frogs.

I spun around. "Yes. It looked like you were closed. So we were leaving."

I knew this motel was not a good place. But it was too late

to keep driving. Too late to get away from this skinny, shy girl. She looked about ten or eleven, with brown eyes and long, dark hair. She wore faded jeans with slits in the knees and a short, tight, yellow tee-shirt that showed her navel.

"My mom is busy with the dogs. I don't think she heard you." She looked down at the cracked sidewalk.

Her voice caught me in its apologetic net, its undertones of neglect and poverty. I glanced at my watch. Ten minutes past one o'clock. *What kind of mother sends a girl into a dark parking lot to speak to strangers in the middle of the night?* I followed her past the blinking lights toward the office door.

The girl opened it wide and a trio of snarling dogs bounded toward me. Short haired and short-tailed, their coats were brindled black, tan, and gray. They had lolling tongues, knobby ears, muscular jaws and shoulders. All three looked as if they gulped steroids with their kibble. I snapped the door shut.

While the girl and her mother corralled the pit bulls, I looked through the window into the large room. It had sparse furniture, one short counter, cardboard boxes and trash littering the floor. A third of the ceiling had collapsed. Judging from the swollen tiles and the vapour barrier hanging down, it looked like water damage. I stared at the piles of rubble, my tired brain clouded by disbelief. *Who would leave an office looking like this? Were they too overwhelmed, too depressed, to clean up the mess? Why couldn't she afford to get the roof fixed?*

The woman yelled and slapped at the dogs. They jumped away, but she cornered them and dragged them into a back room. She waved at me and pointed at the door, to tell me that I should come inside. She must have noticed my hesitation so she opened it, wide.

"Sorry. They're a bit excitable. I'm Jean Turner and this is my daughter Rebecca."

"Oh." I did not want to know the girl's name. It pulled me closer into her sad life.

"We get lots of truckers. And people with pets. They like that they can bring their cats and dogs into the rooms with them."

As if in agreement with her policy, a chorus of barks arose behind the closed door. I tried not to stare at the squashed drink cans, bones, chew toys, pig ears, blankets, and pieces of leather strewn around the floor, behind the counter, in the corners. I inhaled. The room smelled like an over-booked kennel.

Rebecca fumbled with dials on a television in the corner, but no sounds came out.

"We love dogs," Jean said.

"Yeah, I noticed." I turned halfway but did not leave.

She opened a drawer and rummaged around in a nest of papers. At first, I had been too startled by the dogs and the ceiling rubble to notice her appearance. She wore purple sweat pants with a white stripe down the sides, a smudged, pale green smock, and moccasin-style shoes. Dog fur stuck to all surfaces, even the footwear. She had an ashen, thin face, smokers' wrinkles, and bad teeth. Her brown hair, streaked with gray and single-braided, hadn't been cut in years. She looked about fifty-five, but that didn't make sense; it would have meant she had Rebecca in her mid-forties.

She said, "It's been so muggy these past two weeks. We need a good rain to clear the air."

I nodded and thought about the possible effects of "a good rain" on her ceiling. Her smile made me queasy. Her desperate need, almost palpable, kept me in the office.

"How many?" She had found a form.

"Three." *If she got lots of truckers and pet-owners, why was it so hard to find a check-in slip?*

After she wrote a couple of things on it, she passed it to me.

"How much?" I said.

"Forty-five."

This price was another bad sign. I stared at the form and wrote. I blocked out the dogs and the collapsed ceiling, and focused on my children waiting in the car. *After all, how bad could a room be?*

I soon found out. She pulled a key off a hook behind her counter and offered to show me. I followed, cursing myself for being sad and tired and stupid. But I knew it was none of these that made me agree to the room. Before I left the office, I tried to catch Rebecca's attention and make eye contact. To let her know that I understood what it felt like to cope without a husband or father. She just fiddled with the television.

Room number eleven made my eyes sting. The smell of urine brought back not-so-fond memories. During university, for three summers, I had cleaned washrooms in a campground and dealt with every body fluid. I did not want to admit human piss could be embedded in the carpet, so I decided to pretend it was from pets.

When she showed me the washroom, the ammonia smell got stronger. Chunks of plaster and strips of caulking littered the floor. Around the tub, three or four ceramic tiles hung at odd angles, ready to drop if touched. The faded blue shower curtain could not hide the patchwork of stains and mould spots.

I did not bother to look at the beds. Following the woman back to the office to pick up the car and my kids, I reminded myself that we had sleeping bags. We could lay them on top of the blankets. I also reminded myself that even the most misshapen mattresses had to feel more comfortable than a cramped Focus. I passed the streaked office window and saw that Rebecca finally got the television to work.

She lived in this dump. We could stand it for one night.

I got in the car and switched on the ignition, to move it closer to the room. Once again, I watched the mother in the office. She opened the rear door and the dogs tumbled out, barking, whirling, as if they hadn't seen her for days. While she patted them, she pointed at our car and spoke to Rebecca.

The CD started up and Hawksley's voice soared through the last chorus of "Be Clever, not Beautiful."

I said, "She's telling her daughter she did a good job of reeling in another batch of kindhearted, but legally blind, fools."

"What?" said Hanna.

"I said I rented a room so we're going to park in front of it right now."

"This place looks crappy," she said.

"Yeah, but at least it's open."

I looked back at Josh. He squinted at the overhead lights and frowned. "Couldn't we find something better?"

"Maybe not," I said.

At this moment, I thought of their father and hated him. With a huge, seething fury. Although I had enjoyed many parts of the past weekend, the lovebirds at the wedding had ripped open a deep vein of self-pity. On most days, I bore the thorny cross of single parenthood with bitter humour. Here, in the middle of the night, in the middle of nowhere, I wanted to dial some agency and order up another adult to carry the load. I decided not to tell my children about the accordion ceiling in the office until after we left the motel. If I mentioned it now, they might refuse to enter the room.

I thought about Rebecca.

Hanna and Josh reacted to the smell more dramatically than I did. After feigned vomits and loud exclamations, they retrieved their sleeping bags and backpacks from the trunk. They urged me to use the bathroom first. I kept my sandals on, to avoid the crunchy debris. Through the warped door, I heard Josh clicking the television remote. Despite his electronics expertise, he could not get it to work.

I thought about Rebecca again.

I sat on the toilet, stared at dark flecks on the floor and decided they must be mouse turds. While a "hanta virus, hanta virus" chorus played in my head, I grabbed a threadbare towel from the rack, wet it, threw it on the floor and used my foot to mop the linoleum. The towel had a faded Holiday Inn logo. From my days in the janitor business, I knew the filthiest place was always around the toilet. I spent extra time wiping there and flung the towel in the bathtub. None of us would be showering. We were here for the beds.

I stuck a chair against the outside door to allow cooler air to flow inside, but mosquitoes soon discovered the opening. Although Hanna hadn't felt them yet because she was still busy in the bathroom, Josh complained loudly. Swatting them had interrupted his inventory of burnt out and missing light bulbs.

Josh went into the toilet and turned on its squeaking fan.

I retrieved the chair, shut the outside door, and helped Hanna spread out the sleeping bags. After Josh came out of the bathroom, all three of us collapsed on the beds. The fan noise continued for another ten minutes.

The pillows stunk so much I could not fall asleep. I went outside in my nightie and rummaged around in the trunk to retrieve some beach towels to cover them. The light in the main office was turned off.

*No more suckers tonight.*

The smell of sunscreen masked the pillow odours, but our towels could not hide the scent of urine that hung in the air. I turned out the light and said, "I'm sorry. I'm just too tired."

Josh said, "Don't worry. We'll soon be back on the road."

In a few minutes, I heard his soft snores. *He could fall asleep in a hurricane.* I turned on my side and plugged my nose. The tension of the last three hours began to seep out of my shoulders, but I found it difficult to sleep with one hand on my face and my nostrils closed. I released my fingers.

Hanna was not asleep. She shifted in the bed beside me. "Do you think it would be any different if Dad were here?"

"He would have enjoyed the wedding. And he liked your cousins. But I'm never sure. As you know, he didn't like to leave his work. He probably would have stayed at home."

"Yeah, he hated travel. Well, at least now we get to go on holidays."

I laughed. "And stay in piss-infested, sleaze-bag motels."

"It was the little girl, wasn't it?"

Tears stung my eyes. *Was it a hypersensitive reaction to urine or simple fatigue? Or was it the aftermath from his three heart attacks, each one worse than the last, and four years of widowhood?*

"I don't think so." I swallowed the lump in my throat. "Wait. You're right. I felt sorry for that kid. She got to me. "

"And the mother?"

"I admit. I identified with her. Not the skinny-dirty-dog-crazy part. But the living alone part. The trying-to-make-it-work part. With no help to fix things. And no money to pay someone to fix things."

"Are you crying?"

"Yes. The pee stench makes my eyes drip. Soon I'll be drowning in a puddle of my own making."

Hanna shifted the clock radio so she could peer at its numbers. "It's almost two-thirty. If this piece of shit isn't broken."

She turned over and sighed. "I need to get some rest. I work on Tuesday. We don't have to stay here much longer."

I lay in the dark. Sleep did not come. Every fifteen minutes or so, vibrations from the highway shook the walls. The trucks sounded close, as if they might drive over the rear end of our Focus. Each time a big rig roared past, one of the pit bulls started a ruckus. *Maybe they've agreed to take all-night barking shifts.*

I pictured a roof collapsing on my children. Coughed. Swore at the piss sting. And thought about Hanna's last sentence.

"Right. We don't have to stay here much longer," I mumbled into the beach towel.

Hanna moaned and turned over again.

I swung my feet over the edge of the bed and felt around for my sandals. I imagined stepping on one of the mice that inhabited the bathroom. Or one of its turds. I wanted to vomit. But I did not want to use the toilet, even to throw up.

I opened the door and stepped outside. The heat had vanished; a low mist hung around the spruce trees. The white

Focus, the first car I had bought on my own, sat in the rough parking lot, coated with condensation. It had performed well over the vast stretches of boreal highways.

Although the morning air settled my nausea, another wave of grief overwhelmed me. Outside, away from my kids, I let the tears come. *What are we doing here? I'm so angry that we couldn't afford to fly to the wedding, like all my other relatives. What if something happened to me? How would my kids cope? Why do other people have smiling spouses and good jobs and health benefits? I'm tired of feeling poor and unlucky and stressed.*

I cried for about ten minutes, wiped my face with my sweaty nightshirt, and spat into the weedy, dried-up flower bed. Its granite border reminded me that, at one time, this motel must have been a place people wanted to stay. Before the woman lost her mate and had to struggle along on her own. Before the new highway shifted the traffic into the bigger towns, like Huntsville. Or tourist traps like Wasaga Beach.

*At least the ceiling in my house is not falling on my head. At least my kids don't have to solicit strangers in the middle of the night.*

The sun was not yet visible, but burgeoning light coloured the eastern sky. Birds started their pre-dawn chorus. Another semi roared past and a pit bull barked. *As if he needed practice.*

"We don't have to stay here. At all."

For a moment, I considered asking Jean Turner for half of my money back, since we had been in the room for only a couple of hours.

I thought of Rebecca again.

I could not face her, or the dogs. Within ten minutes, we were packed, ready to leave. My children did not protest. They knew I would drive and they could sleep. Hanna reclined in the front and Josh settled in the rear seat, punching at the sleeping bags and pillows around him to create a nest in the cramped space.

"I couldn't stand the smell," I said. We headed back onto the highway.

I reached into the CD case and pulled out the first one in its sleeves. I didn't care if I had heard it ten times already. The music swelled and I heard, once again, the first line of "Sweet Hallelujah."

Hawksley sang, low and sweet. "*This is just a prayer for those who need one.*"

*Damn, you got that right.* I accelerated to cruising speed. If we pushed it and nothing mechanical failed, the Focus would get us back to Manitoba.

# Sam, Lump, and the Boathouse Reno

IT WAS THE FALL OF 1980.

On the last week of June, I had resigned from my teaching position. For the rest of the summer, I worked as a carpenter's helper for a contractor named Steve, in the Many Lakes Provincial Park.

During the spring rush, lake country builders can't find enough time. During the dog days of July, they can't find enough space. Cottage owners like to sit on new docks and decks, not watch them get built — too much sawdust, noise, confusion. But once the cottage people put away water-skis and wakeboards, and close up their cabins, they don't think about renovations. The contractors can spend the following weeks finishing outdoor jobs and catching up, until the snow flies in November.

On August 30, another contractor named Sam approached my friend Steve and asked if he could hire me for a special project. Steve no longer had enough jobs to keep fifteen hired hands busy, so he agreed.

Unlike Steve, Sam worked alone most of the time. However, when he inspected this particular job at Barrett Lake, he realized he could not do it by himself.

He also had four reasons for agreeing to the contract. First off, he needed money for his annual winter trip to Mexico. Second, the cottage sat on a flat lot so he could easily haul in cement, gravel, lumber, and machinery. An accessible job site matters a great deal to builders who often have to load tools and material onto barges or build scaffolds off the sides of cliffs. Third, the client was a retired Mennonite who had just sold his jewellery business. This meant Sam had a better-than-average chance of getting paid. Also, the client promised a big bonus if we finished on schedule.

I did not find out the fourth reason (no one else would do it) until we were well into our second week and up to our armpits in mud and rubble. For Sam, the Menno client personified an ideal father figure and these traits convinced him to take this odd project. A few years earlier, Sam had told me about his childhood as a single son of a single mother.

I remember our first day on this job — September the second, right after the long weekend. Sam picked me up at seven-thirty a.m. in his 1974 GMC half-ton. It was dented, baby blue, with flaking doors and rusted wheel wells. I was staying at my parents' house in order to save money for my upcoming tour of Europe. The parents weren't awake at this hour.

Sam stood six feet tall and had dark blond hair, a full beard, and an easy smile — a giant teddy bear, strong but cuddly. I had only seen him twice since Rick's funeral. Rick was a mutual friend and my former university roommate. He had died the previous winter, of kidney cancer. The weekend after we found out, I went over to Sam's bunkhouse to commiserate. We ended up having comfort sex on his couch. Sam had a long-term girlfriend in the city. When I saw him that first morning, I felt awkward and hot, ashamed that we had betrayed her.

As I slid across the rippled plastic of the bench seat, he asked, "When do you leave?"

"Second week in October. Laura's coming with me." Laura was another mutual friend who taught at the local two-room school.

"We should be done by then." Sam scratched his beard. "Teachers make good money. Why did you quit?"

"I felt trapped by routines and repetitions. Same as Laura. She wants to visit London again, before she settles down."

"That's why I want to head south, for one last trip. Bridget is making noises. We're getting to that age. People get hitched."

I nodded, thought about sex with him, but concentrated on the scenery.

The early sun had burned through the morning mist. Coniferous trees and granite outcrops loomed — ghostly, surreal, incandescent, as if backlit for a movie shot. The clumps of poplar trees had not yet started to change. I could smell their fetid over-ripeness through the slight opening in the truck window. Although night had chilled the boreal forest, it looked like it was going to be another hot day. I regretted not bringing my bathing suit. But Sam had seen me nude. I'd swim without one.

We pulled into the next driveway along highway 32. It led to a rundown old house. I knew the place was seriously dilapidated because it was where I used to live.

After Sam honked the shave-and-a-haircut refrain, he said, "We've stopped here because I hired another person. It's too much for just the two of us."

My eyebrows bunched up in surprise. "Should I be worried?"

"Nah. Three of us can do it."

"I meant about this other helper. Three guys live in that old house and the only one not working for Steve is the one they call Lump. I don't know his real name, but I've heard theories about his nickname."

"I couldn't get anyone else. Steve still needs the two other guys."

"So we got Lump."

"His real name is Paul."

After a couple more honks, Lump appeared in the porch. Then he turned and went back into the house. He reappeared with a metal lunch bucket the size of a small suitcase. He was medium height, broad, sloping shoulders, scruffy stubble, beer gut, reddish brown hair tied in a ponytail. His oversized lunch kit banged against his leg as he walked.

"He must like to eat," I said.

He ambled around the grill of the truck, slapped his open hand on the pockmarked hood and jumped in beside me. I grabbed my backpack off the floor, put it in my lap, and shifted closer to Sam. I smelled Dove soap, mixed with the scent of sweat and day-old pot.

"Did you have a good weekend?" I aimed this remark at Sam because I heard Bridget had visited.

He turned the ignition and started to answer.

Lump interrupted and launched into a long summary of all the parties he had attended over the long weekend. From what I could surmise, Sam and Bridget and Lump had visited a few of the same gatherings. While I sat between these two large men listing all the details of who got wasted and where, who got screwed and where, my head swivelled back and forth. I felt like I was at a tennis match with extra-long rallies. Their intense, but unfocused, conversations set the tone for the next seven weeks.

Sam passed the fish hatchery turn-off and the one-up-manship slowed. The road headed north. As we knocked and swayed over the fifty-year-old pavement, I found out why Lump carried such a huge lunch pail. After about five minutes, he opened the lid, pulled out a plastic bag full of grass, rolled a joint, and stuck it between his lips.

"Anyone want some?" Lump struggled to retrieve his chrome lighter from his jeans' front pocket. I felt his thigh bump against my leg. His belly interfered with access, but he managed to wiggle around enough to get at the lighter. While he sucked on the joint, Sam took his right hand off the steering wheel and reached across my breasts.

"Put your big paw down. I don't want any, but I'll pass it to you."

"Okay, okay. Don't bite."

I handed Sam the lit joint. He took a long drag and then gave it back to me. Lump grabbed it, inhaled as if he had just emerged from a full minute underwater and blew out streams of smoke. H e finished the joint and went to sleep. His snores sounded like a large cat's purring.

Between Lump's wheezing and the half-ton's roaring, Sam and I didn't attempt conversation, even though we were jammed tight against each other. I felt slightly buzzed from second-hand fumes and thought about dozing off, but didn't want to fall onto either guy's shoulders. So I sat up and watched the road unwind. Its unbroken double lines lulled me into a trance.

Twenty minutes later, we reached Barrett Lake. Sam pulled into a narrow lane and stopped his truck, facing a one-story cottage. The cabin sat near the lakeshore, on a level strip of sandy soil. Stumpy jack pines often grow on these ancient beaches, found between granite ridges on the edge of the boreal forest.

In front of the steps, someone had parked a freshly washed, newer model Lincoln Town Car. Its bronze finish reminded me of Swiss chocolate. Lump lurched out of the half-ton and swung the door wide open. I leaped after him to catch it before it smashed into the Lincoln. He did not notice, just yawned and rubbed at his red-rimmed eyes.

Sam got out the driver's side, stood straight and stretched. He looked worse than Lump, sort of rumpled and tired. Maybe Bridget had kept him up all weekend. I felt a sharp stab of jealousy above my left breast, the same one Sam had grazed when he reached for the joint.

*Great*, I thought. Now I was lusting after one and supremely irritated by the other. *Why didn't I buy a plane ticket with a departure date that could be moved forward? Oh yeah, I forgot, Laura needed to work until Thanksgiving, when her replacement teacher appeared. So we could leave together, as planned.*

Right after the truck doors slammed, Sam's prized customer opened the screened entry to the cabin. The man lifted a pale green teacup in his right hand in a kind of a salute, to indicate he wanted us to join him. He wore grey dress pants with a white shirt, open at the neck, no tie, like how a minister might dress, away from the pulpit. He was tall and angular, but round-faced, with a fringe of white hair. He wore thick glasses. Although still alert and upright, he looked at least sixty-five.

Before we reached the steps, a shorter, but much wider, grey-haired woman with glasses joined him. Except for height and width, they looked so much alike they could have been brother and sister. Both wore simple, but expensive, gold watches. The woman carried a similar teacup and waved a welcome. Her dark blue dress framed her face and almost reached the deck boards. Their formal clothing struck me as odd, considering the heat and the setting.

The cabin, like the dress, also hung low to the ground. It had red shingles, new triple-pane windows, and bevelled cedar siding. Otherwise, from the outside, it didn't look too luxurious. A wide veranda wrapped around the waterfront side. The large rear deck, where the couple stood and smiled, faced north toward the parking area.

"I think they want us to come inside." I grinned at Sam as he straightened his denim jacket, ran a hand through his hair, and sniffed his sleeve.

Lump smiled so wide I could see his back fillings. "Don't worry. They're too old and too Mennonite to know what weed smells like. They'll think it's herbs, like rosemary or thyme, that we've eaten in our omelettes."

Turned out he was right. After the couple shook our hands and introduced themselves as Jacob and Esther, they insisted we join them for Earl Grey tea, sweet buns, and homemade rhubarb jam. Lump ate four buns, which made the woman joke about how he must be still growing. She even reached out, as if to pinch his cheek, but stopped herself and touched his massive forearm. This set another precedent; every time she set eyes in him, she hauled out plates of homemade cooking.

While my co-workers chatted with the old couple, I looked around my cabin. Its decor looked Scandinavian. Dining room chairs, tables, rockers, bookshelves were all built of solid teak — elegant and straight-edged. Wide, laminated rafters curved across the open ceiling and matched the furniture and panelled walls.

This use of so much wood spoke "money" to me, but a wealth that didn't want to convey pride or evoke envy. Colourful quilts, rag rugs, and woven hangings lay or hung in various places to counterbalance the dark teak. A huge, leather-bound Bible sat open on an angled table near the couch. There was no television. At least not in the rooms I could see.

A half hour later, after we devoured all the buns, Jacob led us outside to examine the double-door boathouse. Once my eyes adjusted to its dim interior, I realized the job looked much worse than Sam had described. Jacob wanted us to replace his cement boat slip, damaged by age and ice. Thick rebar, twisted and rusted, poked out of the cracked structure. Large slabs of concrete had flaked off the floor deck. Because boulder-sized chunks had fallen into the water, Jacob could no longer park his boat inside the building.

Once he led us back into the sunlight, I understood his concern. He had his boat pulled up on a makeshift ramp, draped with canvas. When he lifted off the cover, Lump and Sam murmured in admiration. Jacob's boat was a vintage wooden inboard with sculptured leather upholstery. Multiple coats of marine varnish had been polished to such a high sheen I could see my reflection. Chrome lights, cleats, windshield brackets, and flag poles gleamed in the harsh fall sunlight.

Jacob patted the mahogany deck. He said, "As you may know, I am a jeweller. I named this beauty the "Lady Diamond," and she's an original Chris Craft. She was first owned by a millionaire banker but she sat in a rotting shed for years while he was sick with cancer. After he died, his family sold their entire island, including cottage, furniture, boats. A cabinetmaker in Kenora restored her to her former glory. She needs to be inside for the winter."

Like a raven, entranced by shiny bits, Lump chirped and stroked the chrome. His buttery fingers left smeared prints. Good thing Jacob turned back with Sam to discuss the excavation. Or he might have slapped Lump for desecrating his beloved Lady.

By noon, we had dug a metre-wide ditch along the rear wall, where the building was set into the sloping shore. The soil was a sandy loam, but we discovered plenty of boulders and pine roots. Although we were busy heaving rocks and throwing dirt out of the chest-deep trench, Lump somehow managed to keep a roach going, like an old geezer with a lit cigarette dangling from his lip. In such tight quarters, once again, the second-hand smoke gave me a slight buzz. Sam helped us shovel, but often climbed out to go talk to Jacob, then reappeared to let us know what the old man wanted.

At precisely twelve o'clock, Esther's round head popped over the edge of the trench to invite us to lunch. This meal established another habit. Every second or third day, they drove out from Winnipeg. Jacob would meet with Sam and check on our progress, and Esther would cook up a huge spread.

At lunch, she smiled and cooed at our bright-eyed Lump. "Oh yes, I grew up on a farm, east of Grothwell. Since I was twelve, I helped my mother feed combine crews. This job brings back such memories. Cooking for men." She looked at me, in my dirty jeans, tee-shirt, long ponytail. "But never for a girl. The women stayed in the kitchen."

Other than these wistful comments, she did not treat me with disdain, but rather like a three-legged dog — to be pitied, but still lovable, and feedable. At these meals, she handed out tea and casseroles and pies, and spoke politely to Jacob and Sam, or sat and listened to their theories about the boathouse's structural capabilities. But it was Lump's stoned affability and giant appetite that loosened her tongue. She often turned to him, urged him to eat, and teased about finding him a nice

Mennonite girl. I found it strange that a jeweller's wife did not comment on his multiple earrings, some fashioned out of bent nails.

During lunches, Lump warmed to her overtures and joked back. He played the part of the big, strong son she never had. Unfortunately, this hour of animation wore him out. After lunch, he fell asleep on the truck seat, or, if Sam had to pick up more lumber or cement, he flopped down on a pile of old canvas, out of sight, behind the beautiful wooden boat. While he slept, I dug. I resented his lack of commitment, but welcomed the chance to draw a fresh breath.

After a couple of days, I realized that Jacob wanted us to tear out the ruined cement slip and somehow preserve the three half-walls, rafters, and roof of the boathouse. To me, it looked easier, and cheaper, to rip apart the whole structure and start from scratch, but I was a mere woman, not a contractor. While I shovelled, alone, I fumed and vacillated between the idea that Jacob was a cheap-ass swindler who thought he could save money by preserving the top half of a decrepit boathouse and the idea that Sam was a cheap-ass swindler who had found an easy mark, an old man who would witness how hard we worked and pay us, no matter how long this job took.

After a week, we had trenched around the entire foundation. Sam borrowed a jackhammer from a contractor in East Lake and set Lump to work on breaking up the remaining floor and sides of the slip. Although Lump donned a set of ear protectors and safety goggles, he still kept his joints lit. While he sweated and jiggled, I swung a sledge hammer and shovelled all the concrete chunks into a wheel barrow. We removed our pants and lifted stray pieces out of the lake. I carried them off and poured them behind the riprap, to reinforce the shoreline on both sides of the boathouse. Then we jacked up the top half, the wooden part of the structure, and suspended it on an intricate web of beams and timbers.

After two weeks, Sam realized what little progress we had

made and how hard it was to work in such close confines, dodging rebar and supports. Despite the slip's crumbled surfaces, it resisted our efforts to break it apart. Lump even fell into the lake three times, but I couldn't tell if that was because of the crowded conditions, the dust inside the boathouse, or the fact he was stoned. Every time, he managed to keep the jackhammer dry by lifting it up over his shoulders. A dangerous move, in my opinion, but his head remained intact.

Also, Esther loved making elaborate meals of noodles, borscht, cookies, and cheesecake for her beloved "Brother Paul," as she called him. These treats slowed us down almost as much as the stubborn cement. After lunch, Lump slept much longer than usual, as if in a coma, behind the Lady Diamond.

Some days, Sam helped us dig and chip, but other times, we did not see him for hours.

On the Monday morning of the last week in September, he showed up at my house with his truck full of sheets of used plywood, old tires, and a wooden box wrapped in canvas. After Lump got in the truck, Sam looked over at both of us. "Do either of you know anything about dynamite?"

Lump yelped for joy and slapped his thighs.

"What?" I said.

"I bought a couple dozen sticks of dynamite from Johnny Sawka."

"The mad trapper?" I attempted to picture John's pocked and hairy face, but he didn't come to town often so the image came up blurred.

"Yep. From Longbow Lake. He gets paid to blow up beaver dams. When their ponds flood the subdivision roads."

"Don't you need a license?" I tried not to sound too school-marm-ish as I turned to look at the box bouncing around in the back of the truck. Lump fumbled around to light his joint, smiled at me, and, like a thirsty baby, sucked on his toke.

Although most of the pavement on the road to Barrett Lake looked as if it had been strafed by bazookas, Sam drove his usual speed. He said, "Maybe. But John showed me the basics. And no one will hear or see us. Most days, this late in the fall, there's nobody around."

He was right; the tourists had left. We never saw any other cottage owners, only Jacob and Esther. The south end of the lake was deserted. Even the Barrett Lake store had shut down for the winter. If we wanted a drink or a meal, we had to drive five kilometres back to East Lake.

Lump blew out and spoke in his squeaked-out voice. "We'll have to do it when they aren't feeding us. Jacob will throw a shit fit if you blow the roof off his beloved boathouse."

Sam laughed. "I don't plan to. I just want to blast that stubborn cement to pieces. It's taking forever doing it by hand."

"Even with the jackhammer?" Lump asked.

"Yes, even with the jackhammer. I've heard old concrete gets stronger, especially when it's submerged in water. " Sam held out his fingers, took the fat joint from Lump, and pulled in a long toke.

I said, "Better not let any pieces land on the Lady Diamond. I think he loves it more than his damn boathouse. Or his dumpling wife."

At that moment, I wanted Sam to turn around and take me home. Handling dynamite with two potheads unsettled me. For the remainder of the drive, I prayed that Jacob and Esther would pick today for a visit. As we bounced along, I tried to remember if they preferred sunny days or cooler days.

When we pulled into the parking lot, the Lincoln was not in sight. Sam bounded out of the truck, excited by the prospect of finally getting rid of the boathouse floor. He had planned to finish by the end of September, but we hadn't even started to pour the new cement.

While he unloaded the box of dynamite, Lump and I lugged the plywood down to the waterfront. They had been used as forms for foundations and basements so they were torn at the edges, grey and heavy, full of nails, coated with layers of cement. I counted the sheets as we carried them through the boathouse doorway, now much wider. How did Sam know how many it took to absorb a blast inside a small building?

If Lump shared my concerns, he did not show it. As we laid the sheets against the pony wall, he whistled and grinned. Since we had started this job, his long silences made him a cipher to me. He only came alive when Esther showed up. I couldn't tell if it was her calorific meals or the hugs and cheek pinches. Or the fact that she always called him Brother Paul.

While we fetched the ragged tires, Sam used a cement drill to bore holes for the dynamite. I excused myself to the outhouse when he started to push the sticks into the holes. I did not return until he had the fuses attached. We layered the sheets of plywood over all the cement surfaces and spread the used tires on top. The pile reached almost up to the rafters.

Lump stood up straight and rubbed his lower back. "Hey, boss, are you sure you know what you're doing?"

He said this in his characteristic drawl, nonchalant and half-ripped. But it was the one question I wanted to ask. Sam nodded and grinned. Sweat and cement dust had darkened his broad forehead. Layers of mud had settled in its creases and highlighted the wrinkles around his eyes. He wiped his sleeve across his face and laughed.

"Yes, of course."

That's when we heard the distinctive V-8 growls of Jacob's Town Car driving up the narrow lane.

Sam jumped to the opening where the door used to be. "Christ! He didn't say he was coming out!"

Lump giggled, and, without a word, exited the boathouse and headed toward the cottage. Sam grabbed a spare sheet of plywood. He motioned me to hold the end while he grabbed nails and a hammer from his pouch and tacked it across the opening.

"Doesn't Jacob usually tell you?" I asked. "Or does he like to surprise you?"

"Depends. But I sure as hell don't want him to see this." He grunted as he worked. "Lump is like one of Pavlov's dogs. He started to drool as soon as heard the car. I think he plans to head Esther off at the kitchen. Once he gets her talking about food, she'll call us for lunch."

"I think he has rhubarb pie radar."

Sam snorted. "I just need him to keep Jacob away from the boathouse."

"I can understand why."

Whatever Brother Paul did or said worked. In ten minutes, Esther called us to the cottage.

Sam and I washed up for lunch in the peaches-and-cream bathroom while Lump sat in the kitchen and teased and laughed and complimented her on the smells bubbling out of the pots and oven. She had prepared potatoes in a cream sauce, with spicy sauerkraut and homemade sausage on the side. Jacob greeted us and we all sat down at the teak table. As usual, after Esther ladled out her massive portions, Jacob launched into a lengthy grace.

"May God bless all who are about to share your bounty, gathered here in this peaceful forest."

I struggled to suppress a snicker. Sam had shoved at least forty sticks of dynamite into Jacob's boat slip. Peaceful, my ass.

"We pray for these talented workers, who laboured long and hard to do our bidding. With God's help, they will repair the damage wrought upon our special place. And they will restore our blessed retreat to its former beauty and glory."

I bit my lip and opened my eyes. Sam smiled and stared at me. He clutched my forearm to stifle my laughter, and his own. Lump had folded his hands, but his head hung down so low his stubbly beard almost brushed the sauce, as if he wanted to vacuum up the food. When Jacob's voice signalled he had built up to his finale, Esther sighed. I glanced at her pinched eyes and beatific smile. Her face shone with a matriarch's kitchen pride.

After we finished lunch, Sam somehow convinced Jacob it was too dangerous to poke around in the rubble so the old couple packed up without inspecting our progress. Around one o'clock, we waved goodbye to them and walked down the slope to the boathouse.

Sam grinned as he checked the fuses one final time. Then he pulled out his lighter and lit them.

He said, "Let's go sit in the truck."

Both men turned and sprinted toward the parking lot.

I had never seen either one move so fast so I figured they must know something — like how much damage flying chunks of concrete can inflict. We all piled into the half-ton, breathless and sweaty, and slammed the doors. We didn't have to wait long.

A low rumbling echoed across the lake and rippled, in waves, up the hill to the truck. I glanced over my shoulder at the boathouse and saw giant clouds of dust emerge from all its openings, large and small, known and unknown. The building looked like it was on fire. We waited, speechless, to make sure all the sticks had exploded. The dust drifted away, in a low cloud floating across the flat water.

Sam said, "It's probably finished."

"What do you mean, 'probably'?" I said.

Lump whistled and pounded the dash. "Hope there aren't any tourists around. They'll be calling the RCMP any minute."

Sam opened the door, squinted, and cocked his head, as if he expected more explosions, racing engines, sirens, or other loud noises. "Yeah, make sure you hide your stash."

"I guess you won't need your afternoon nap," I said to Lump.

He slid off the cracked seats and patted his stomach. "Yeah, lots to digest, but way too much excitement."

We laughed and headed down the hill to the boathouse. The dynamite had done its work; the cement was shattered into tiny pieces. Dust still hung in the air. Sam and Lump slapped each other's backs and gave high-fives.

The explosion had torn the plywood sheets into tattered

strips and shredded most of the tires, but it only ripped a few large splinters out of the rafters. We counted about twenty dents and what looked like bullet holes in the walls. Sam said he could repair them before Jacob came out again. We worked all afternoon to clear out the rubble. No one showed up to investigate the noise.

THE NEXT WEEK, THE WEATHER CHANGED. Along the road to Barrett Lake, the poplars, which had blazed yellow for the past two weeks, began to surrender their leaves, bowing under the onslaught of a fierce northern wind.

For two days, we built forms for the new foundation and the slip. Jacob and Esther did not appear. Intermittent bouts of rain tore up the surface of the lake, frothed by the snappy breeze. Lump and Sam no longer stripped off their shirts to work.

While we cut and hammered, I thought about the weather in Greece and how glad I was to be inside the boathouse, out of the driving wet. Lump continued to smoke up, but he did not take so many naps. Thousands of geese gathered on the water, lured by the troughs of grain at the nearby goose sanctuary. At times, their honking overwhelmed our conversations. When Sam went for lumber, Lump and I didn't talk much. We only chatted at lunch, huddled together inside the boathouse and bent over our lunch kits. Once the sweaty warmth of constant movement dissipated, it left us chilled and damp. This gave us incentive to get back to work. Our breaks were short and purposeful, unlike the long, heavy lunches with Jacob and Esther.

The days rolled by and we absorbed Sam's urgency to complete the job. In the middle of the next week, he showed up with a cement mixer in the back of his truck. The rain had let up; an anaemic sun poked through the clouds. It smelt like snow.

Before we picked up Lump, Sam turned to me, smiled and said, "Time to get that sucker done. I've ordered two truckloads of gravel. We can pour today."

"I hope the rain stays away."

"It had better. We're already taking two weeks longer than I planned. I never thought it would be so hard to smash up that old slip."

"Or refuse lunchtime interruptions."

"Yeah, I think Jacob and Esther are lonely. I hope he agrees to pay for the extra work. My estimate was at least fifty per cent too low."

"And how could you have known Lump needed so much sleep?"

"Right. But he's my ace in the hole. Esther adores him."

I nodded and smiled back and wondered if Bridget was coming out on the weekend. I felt as isolated and peevish as a teenager, living at home with my parents. I could not wait to leave.

All day, we poured cement.

Every fifteen minutes or so, Lump and I shovelled in a mixture of gravel, water and powder, and watched it blend together. Then one of us would dump the wet muck into Sam's wheelbarrow, he'd roll it down to the boat house and slosh it into the forms. While he coaxed this slurry into every corner of the new slip, we'd throw another batch into the cement mixer.

In keeping with Sam's track record of underestimates, we needed four more bags of cement so he had to drive back to East Lake. And two truckloads of gravel were not quite enough. By the end of the afternoon, Lump had resorted to scraping up grit from the parking lot.

"I hope Jacob doesn't notice all the moss and twigs," I said.

Lump threw in another shovelful of dirty gravel. "He'll be dead, anyway, by the time his new slip falls apart. Besides, who would haul us another load, out in the bush, so late in the day? Now we've started, we have to finish."

While we mixed up the last of the cement, Sam smoothed out the new boathouse floor. His feelings of being rushed spread to us, and did not bode well for the size and complexity of the U-shaped wooden forms, set halfway in the water. It was almost dark by the time we finished. On the silent ride home, these feelings of defeat and dread did not go away.

The next day, we found out why. One of the forms on the right side had given way. The new slip curved outward, in an ugly arc, almost an arm's length into the lake. We stared in disbelief at the bend in the concrete.

Lump pulled out a joint and lit it. "Holy shit! Jacob will crap his pants. That damn bulge might scratch his Lady Diamond."

Sam spat into the water and ran his hands through his curls. "Well, I sure as hell don't feel like hammering that apart. Especial since it's underwater. Jacob is going to have to learn to live with it."

I said, "It reminds me of those churches and buildings that Barcelona architect made. You know, Gaudi — all freeform, organic shapes. I plan to go see them. "

"Oh yeah, when does your plane leave? Maybe I'll come along. To escape the wrath of the righteous."

My heart did a flip under my sternum. "Just six more days. I heard Laura is raring to go."

Lump sucked long and hard, and looked at Sam. "Jacob's a God-fearing man. He won't hurt you."

Sam reached over and took the joint from Lump. "He might refuse to pay. And God-fearing men have long memories. He might even sue."

We spent the rest of the day dismantling the forms, picking up rebar, tires, plywood, and garbage. Then we loaded up the truck with the hand tools and debris from the dynamite experiment.

A stiff breeze chilled our many trips up and down the hill, back and forth from the boathouse. The wind stirred up the lake and sent bands of mist streaming off the cooling mass. It stripped off the last of the poplar leaves and spun them across the surface of the water.

The new, stark shapes of these trees suited our unspoken sense of failure in this place where we had started out in such golden hope, on the bright day that now seemed months ago. No more rides in the cozy cab, wedged between two bulky men, rolling down the shattered highway. No more mornings spent tossing shovelfuls of dirt. No more dips in the lake, after overheating under the fall sun. No more giant meals with the smothering Esther. One last time, we drove away from the pine-shaded parking lot.

THREE DAYS LATER, on the Friday of the Thanksgiving weekend, our friends hosted a going-away party for Laura and me. Both Lump and Sam showed up, along with Steve and most of his crew. The guys chatted and joked about "the God-Squad Job from Hell." Sam looked embarrassed and swallowed half a bottle of Scotch to hide his discomfort. The party lasted until the morning hours and deteriorated into a boozy, boisterous din. Around two a.m., Sam sidled up to me. A salacious grin unfolded across his wide features. I thought he might want sex so my heart did another flip in my chest.

"It turned out okay," he said.

Four beers, a pounding Doors album, and his drunken slur confused me. "What?"

"With Jacob. I met him and Esther at their cottage the day after we left. She fed me, but dragged around in the kitchen like a dog that had lost his master. She wanted to see Lump; she wanted to say good-bye to him."

"Jacob paid you?"

"Yeah, after I explained at length how hard it was to finish. He said he understood. Even gave me a bonus. But he didn't look pleased about the holes in his siding and the wow in his boat slip."

"Can't say I blame him."

"Thanks for your help. That was a tough job. Have a good time in Europe."

"You're welcome. I will. It was fun, in a weird way."

He turned to leave. "I need to go. Bridget's coming out tomorrow. Can't be too hung over."

"Right."

AND THAT WAS HOW IT ENDED. After that drunken night, I never saw Sam or Lump again.

I backpacked around Europe for six months. When I returned, they had both left to work in the city. Through conversations with Steve, I learned that Sam had married Bridget and Lump had moved in with a newly divorced woman whose biker ex-husband threatened to kill him.

I also never saw Jacob or Esther again.

Three Septembers after I returned from my trip, I drove past their narrow driveway, nestled amongst the pines, and saw a Woodland Realty sign. It was a warm fall night and I considered pulling off the road to check it out, but I was in a hurry to get home and mark English essays. Instead, I stopped in at the Barrett Lake Store and asked about the cottage. The owner told me Esther had died recently so Jacob decided to sell it.

Whenever I drive past the giant billboard on highway 95, advertising their former, but still-successful jewellery store, I think about Jacob and Esther. On those rare occasions when I see a vintage boat tied to a dock or zipping across open water, I compare it to the gleaming Lady Diamond.

Every time I drive the winding highway through the Many Lakes Provincial Park, I think of Sam and Lump. I remember the smell of marijuana, the echoing rumble of dynamite, the heavy Mennonite lunches, and the long hours we spent pounding on unyielding cement.

Last summer, I ran into Steve and he told me that Sam died from a heart attack. I missed both the obituary and the funeral. I have often wanted to stop at the cottage on Barrett Lake and check if the boat slip has held up. But I haven't done it yet.

# Ditched

IT WAS THE SECOND WEEK OF APRIL, A COOL AND RAINY FRIDAY.
It had poured on and off for three days. But Adam Tucker
didn't care. He was finished work for the day and planned to
attend a weekend writers' workshop at the luxurious Wolf
Lake Resort in Granite Ridge Provincial Park. After he loaded
his Toyota Corolla with books, guitar, clothing, and footwear
for both winter and spring weather, he headed south on highway 215.

It had been a wet spring — snowy, cold, slow to arrive.
Across the flatlands of Manitoba, the Red River and its tribu-
taries dragged houses, sheds, and trees northward to Lake
Winnipeg. The southern plains spent weeks underwater. But
the eastern edge of Manitoba missed the worst of it — just
some overland flooding and soggy fields. In the small community of Biscuit Lake, where Adam lived, the levels in the
Greenwood River did not rise much above usual.

His home had not been affected by the spring runoff, but he
felt more and more exasperated by the irony of so much water
flowing where it wasn't wanted.

Last September, he had rented a small riverside cabin and
now it had no functional plumbing. In January, after three
weeks of temperatures hovering around minus forty, the shore
ice near his rented cabin had frozen solid, right to the bottom.
The waterline under the nearby dock stopped pulling water.
When he contacted his landlord, Larry Crow, the man insisted
it had never happened before.

Adam glanced at his watch. The light rain had turned into heavy pellets clattering on the windshield. This close to the edge of town, the speed limit remained seventy kilometres per hour, but he pressed his foot harder on the accelerator. He wanted to get to Granite Ridge before dark.

When Mike Gauthier, Adam's next-door neighbour, found out about the waterline crisis, he'd said, "Here's the key to my old farmhouse. You can shower there. Every day, if you want. Saves me going out there to check on it."

Adam remembered the exact date his cabin's waterline froze — January twenty-sixth, the Sunday after his son Devon's second birthday. He'd driven into Winnipeg for a rare visit with the toddler.

He had arrived back at his cabin the next morning and the temperature had risen to minus thirty-five. He lit the wood stove, pissed, and turned on the tap to wash his hands. Only a spurt of air and a dribble of water came out. The pump ran and shut off, ran and shut off, but no more water appeared.

Weeks later, after dozens of phone calls and visits by random plumbers, Adam had resigned himself to hauling four-litre jugs of water, and smelling fermented urine in the toilet bowl. He let it accumulate because he used his water sparingly and didn't want to pour precious liquid down the toilet. So he flushed it with the contents of one large blue jug, only once or twice a day. He couldn't invite people to visit, but received plenty of offers of washing machines and bathrooms. The cabin remained silent — no whir of pump, no burble of water heater, and no swoosh of UV filter. Whenever a log dropped in the stove, he jumped, startled by its sharp clunk against the metal.

About a half a kilometre from Mike's farmhouse, Adam accelerated out of a long curve. That's when he saw the boy. Off in the distance, a slim youth in a grey hoodie, stumbling along the shoulder of the highway.

At almost the same instant, in the shadow of a pine tree, he spotted a dark-haired woman walking between his car and the teenager, on the opposite side of the road. These twin sightings of human activity surprised him. Highway 215 had very little traffic, except in the summer, when hordes of tourists rushed to their cottages. In all the weeks he'd been using Mike's shower, he'd never seen any pedestrians.

Dressed in bright green rain pants and jacket, the dark-haired woman looked determined, as if she went for a walk every day, rain or sun, for exercise.

Adam slowed as she strode toward him. Then she flagged him down.

After he rolled down his window, she leaned against the side of his car and smiled at him. Medium build with short legs, she wore a knitted yellow headband that covered her ears and held back her damp curls. He didn't know her name, but her face was familiar. He could say this about almost everyone in Biscuit Lake. One side of her lips was pulled up by an old injury. It looked as if she grinned at the world, a cock-eyed half-smile, all the time.

She said, "Hi, I'm Sylvia Muldrew."

He extended his hand. "Adam Tucker."

She returned his grip, firm and quick, not too strong. She pointed at the teenager. "See that kid up there. He keeps falling. I've been watching him for a while, but I'm afraid to get closer. I don't know him."

As they both looked up the road, the youth tripped and slid off the narrow edge of the shoulder. He didn't even put out his hands to stop his fall and he landed in fast-moving water. After the boy splashed around a bit, he dragged himself upright on the brown grass and continued on his way.

"I'll check on him. I know that kid."

Her lopsided mouth blew out a sigh of relief and she grinned again. "Okay, I'll stay here. And call the cops if he causes any trouble."

Adam had lied. He wasn't sure if he knew him. But the kid had stumbled in between him and his shower, so he felt obligated, as if he couldn't pass by without helping. And the woman had asked for his assistance.

He drove closer and slowed to a stop. "Are you all right?"

The boy turned and looked and almost lost his balance again. "Yeah, I'm okay." He kept walking.

"Do you need a ride?"

The boy hesitated, turned and looked again; he stared at his wet knees and looked up at the sky and considered the options. "Yeah, that would be good."

He stumbled around the front of the Toyota, put his hand out and leaned on its hood. Then he climbed inside. As he groped around to find and fasten the seat belt, Sylvia walked up and asked, "Is everything okay?"

Adam smiled at her.

"I know him." This time it was true. Once the boy was up close and in the car, Adam recognized him.

Sylvie strode away from Adam's car, back to the clump of houses on the edge of town.

Adam said, "Your name's Mark, right?"

The boy nodded and hunched forward.

Adam thought, *Maybe he wants to vomit but maybe he also wants to hide the reek of hard liquor.* Mark pulled his hoodie tight around his face, as if to smother the smell.

"You're drunk, aren't you?" Adam said.

Now that he had nothing to hide, Mark nodded again and sat up straighter. The hoodie fell away from his face, but he did not look at Adam. Instead, he jammed his wet hands in his soaked kangaroo pocket and stared across the dash, down the empty road he had been determined to follow. Adam shifted into gear and drove off, alternating between looking at the road and looking at the boy's face. Limp, dark blond hair hung around his cheeks. He looked anaemic, pale and fragile, not much muscle on his bones. Adam examined the sharp angles of his cheeks and tried to remember how old Mark was.

"Your mom's Cathy?"

Another nod.

"And she works at the Pinewood Bar and Grill?"

Another nod.

"Do you want to go home? Or to your grandma's house?"

Vigorous shake. "I'm going to work. That's where I was headed."

"Oh yeah? Your boss won't mind?"

Mark shook his head. "He'll make sure I'm okay."

"And who's your boss?"

Mark pointed and slumped back a bit, as if exhausted at the thought of working, drunk and wet. "Doug Bannister. He lives up there, on Hudson Road."

Adam knew Mark's boss, by name and by sight, at least. Mid-forties, tall, with longish, dark hair. Doug's family owned a sprawling two-story lodge and a small farm, upriver of Adam's cabin. Whenever he went for his showers at Mike's farmhouse, he drove by the Bannister place.

"Have you graduated yet?" Adam didn't need to know Mark's age. But he wanted to keep him talking so he wouldn't pass out in the car.

"No. School doesn't work for me. I'm only fifteen and a half. I can't drop out yet. But I don't go to classes much."

Mark only filled about half of the passenger seat. Hunched over again, he had started to shiver. Adam wanted to stop the car and wrap him in the sleeping bag he carried in the trunk, to ward off hypothermia. Instead, he patted the top of the boy's hoodie. *A dumb move*, he thought, but the teenager bent his head under his fingers, as if he accepted the intent of the gesture. Like a Labrador retriever, starved for attention.

Adam put his hand back on the wheel. "Your sister's been out of high school for a couple of years, right?"

"Yeah, she cooks at Chicken Delight."

"Does your mom still live in the old house beside your

grandma's place?"

"Yeah. Her boyfriend works at the mine. We were going to move in with him. But he knocked her around."

"Sorry about your grandpa." Adam glanced at Mark.

Adam wrote for and edited the regional newspaper, the Biscuit Lake Journal, so people supplied him with plenty of unsolicited information. Perhaps more than he needed to do his job. That's how he knew about Doug and Cathy and almost everyone else in town, even though he'd only lived in the area for less than ten months.

Two years earlier, Mark's grandfather had ordered a ready-to-move house and set it up on his farmyard, in front of the old barns, bins, and corrals. Last October, when his wiry farmer's body started to fall apart from cancer, he went out to the workshop and shot himself with the same .22 calibre rifle he'd used to kill skunks and coyotes.

Mark ducked his head back into his hoodie and inhaled deeply. Then he shuddered. Adam worried again about Mark slipping into hypothermia or throwing up on the dash, but the boy only leaned back into the seat.

They travelled a few minutes in silence. Then Mark sat up and pointed. "That's where I work, up ahead."

Adam turned left at Hudson Road, which served as sort of a main driveway to the Bannister enclave. Only a couple of other summer residents used this narrow lane for access to their riverside cottages. As they bumped along on the uneven gravel, Adam wondered how the Bannister family had managed to hold on to this much waterfront property.

When they had almost reached the river, Mark pointed to a towering archway of peeled logs. A heavy, carved sign hung in its middle and read "Bannister Farms." The letters, painted bright green and red, bulged out from a tartan background. At either end, two Charolaise bulls crouched, as if ready to charge each other.

Adam slowed the Toyota. *Mark's grandfather wouldn't have*

*spent money on such a fancy sign. In fact, not many farmers around here would have bothered.*

From the driveway, a Dodge Ram pick-up appeared; its bulbous, bright cherry hood glistened amongst the drab poplars. The brawny fenders made Adam think of the bulls on the sign. He slowed the car and looked over at Mark to check if he knew the driver.

"It's him!" A quick smile lit the boy's blanched features. He did not wait until Adam stopped the car before he unbuckled and opened the door. He paused, after his rush to get out, and spoke over his shoulder. "Thanks for the ride."

Mark headed toward the truck. He still wobbled, but moved with speed and conviction. When he reached the driver's door, the man rolled down the window and said a few words. Mark ran around to the passenger side. As he swung the wide door and mounted the chrome step, he stumbled backward. For a second, Adam thought he might drop into the willows on the edge of the road, but Mark righted himself and climbed inside. Adam thought he saw the driver grab Mark in his arms and embrace him. Silhouettes of heads and shoulders disappeared for a couple of minutes.

Adam assumed the adult in the truck was Mark's boss, but, from such a distance, he couldn't be sure. He watched as the two of them sat up and conversed. He considered driving up to the truck to tell Doug about the boy's drunkenness. Then he turned on the radio and waited for them to drive past him. But the Ram half-ton reversed out of sight, back into the thicket of grey poplars.

After the truck disappeared, Adam swore and slapped his forehead. He had almost forgotten. He still needed a shower. He wanted to arrive on time at the start of the workshop, preferably clean and shaved, for the introductions and meet-and-greet. The gravel road was narrow and he could not see any place to turn around, so he backed the hundred metres to the main road and turned left on highway 215.

WHILE ADAM DROVE to Granite Ridge Provincial Park, through the lakes and swamps and rock outcrops, he had time to think about what had happened. *Why was Mark so falling-down-drunk during a school day? Did ever I get so wrecked when I was that age? Why would a young guy jump into a truck and hug his boss? What exactly did I see back there?*

Then he thought about Devon's birthday. And how much he sucked at being a father.

After his girlfriend, Valerie, found out she was pregnant, she told Adam she wanted to keep the baby. Her voice had sounded thin and flat, but determined. He didn't know what to say.

She had continued, despite his non-response. "Mom's retired now so she can babysit. It's been lonely for her since Dad died."

He had felt a stab of guilt.

Devon's birth had not altered his life. Adam had continued at university, got a degree in political science, and then went into journalism. His first job as a reporter brought him to Biscuit Lake. He'd regretted moving so far north, but figured it didn't matter.

Despite his failure to send a sympathy card, and his ongoing neglect of his son, Adam had visited Devon for his second birthday and shared a cake with Val's family. After Val's mother and Devon went to bed, he drank two bottles of wine with Val. She had agreed that it was too cold and Adam was too drunk to drive back to Biscuit Lake so he could sleep over. But she'd said "No way in hell!" when he asked if she wanted to have sex.

Adam could not think about Devon without doubting his choices. *What could I have done differently? Asked her to marry me? She's the one who refused to get an abortion. She's the one who didn't give a shit about finishing her degree.*

It was almost seven o'clock. Despite the waning light and a road that wound so much it had only solid double lines, he stomped on the gas pedal.

He did not see the red fox until it was too late. It ran into the Corolla's path, and, with a burst of speed, almost made it across the road. Adam swerved and braked, but his left fender clipped its hindquarters. The impact made a dull splat like a slab of beef slamming onto a wooden table. The last thing Adam saw was the white-tipped tail, arcing out of the cone of light created by his headlights, as the animal tumbled head-over-heels off the steep edge of the road.

He stopped his car and got out. He looked up at the quiet sky and shouted a string of profanities. Then he stopped swearing and listened. The fox panted and whined, thrashing around in the bulrushes, but he did not dare approach it. For about fifteen minutes, he stood on the narrow road, shivering, until he no longer heard it moving.

He stared into the darkness.

A sudden screech ripped through the silent forest — long and raw and piercing. For another minute, he stood and peered at the wall of trees. Then he remembered. He'd heard about this kind of shriek from a friend who raised small livestock for fur and meat. But he'd never experienced it. Somewhere in the bushes near the road, a rabbit had been captured by a predator, perhaps the dead fox's mate.

After he checked his fender for damage, he looked at his watch and got into the Corolla. He drove the rest of the way to the Wolf Lake Resort ten kilometres under the speed limit. Braking at every shrub and tree stump near the road, he imagined deer, moose, bears, and wolves lurking in the forest, poised to jump in front of his car. He was already late; he did not want to park at any of the picnic sites and nap for half an hour.

In both directions, no vehicles of any kind passed him.

A WEEK LATER, outside the Biscuit Lake post office, Adam saw the woman who had stopped him on highway 215. He had asked around and had found out she was a massage therapist at the Biscuit Lake Health Centre, married to the recently-hired Anglican minister.

Sylvia stopped directly in front of him and said, "What happened?"

Adam had to think before he answered. "I took him to his boss. Mark got into his big red truck and they drove away. I never heard anything else."

"I heard he went to Preston."

Adam thought harder. *Was she referring to Mark or his boss?* "Do you mean he's going to school there?"

"No, he's staying on a ward. He tried to kill himself, with his grandfather's gun."

The nearest mental hospital was located in a town, about fifty kilometres away, called Preston. "Gone to Preston" was a code phrase used by locals to describe someone admitted for mental health problems. Or committed.

"Oh."

"Well, I hope he gets some help."

"Right."

Three weeks later, Adam spotted the Ram half-ton parked in front of the same post office. Mark sat low, almost invisible behind the padded dash, slouched in the passenger seat. Adam looked around for Doug. Then he walked over to the truck and circled his index finger to indicate that he wanted Mark to roll down the window.

Mark pushed the button, sat up straighter and squinted at Adam, his eyes not showing any flickers of recognition. The boy's face looked parched and thinner, his skin as translucent as a deep-sea creature, except around his eyes, where dark smudges stood out against his pale face.

His jaw tightened and his lips set into an obstinate line. "What do you want? Doug's not here. He went to buy a sump pump at Home Hardware."

"That's okay. I wanted to talk to you."

Mark's eyes squinted even narrower and still showed no

signs of recognizing Adam. He shifted in his seat, turned away and looked down the street, as if searching for Doug, as if telepathically pleading with him to come back right away, to end this unwelcome conversation.

Adam smiled what he hoped was an encouraging grin. "Do you remember me? I picked you up about a month ago. You'd fallen in the ditch near Marshall Road. I gave you a ride."

A memory of this event, however blurred, seemed to take hold and alter the suspicious look in the boy's eyes. He lowered his gaze and examined his closely chewed fingernails. "Oh yeah, I was messed-up that day. Doug told me about it later. I don't remember much except being soaked."

Standing by the truck in the spring sun, Adam felt a rush of urgency. Mark looked ready to roll up the window. Before he lost his chance, Adam wanted to help this kid, to give him some adult advice, to set him on a different path.

Instead, he said, "I hope you're okay."

Mark looked up again. He did not squint at Adam; he opened his eyes wide. But they held no emotion, as if some kind of cold emptiness had settled behind the pupils.

Adam thought he could see the curtain drop. *What was that word that word psychologists used? Dissociation.*

"Don't worry. I'm okay. Doug will take care of me. He always does."

The window glass slid up, before Adam could respond. Then Mark pulled his hoodie strings tight to hide his face and slumped down in his seat.

Adam stared at Mark, but the boy did not look up.

*What the hell was going on?*

Adam thought he'd done the right thing. Although he was a newcomer to this backwoods shithole, he'd picked Mark up when he was stumbling drunk and falling into ditches. He had deposited him with another ostensibly responsible adult and driven away.

*But what was the right thing to do when I had no proof, only a hunch?*

Adam spotted Doug in the distance, about half a block away. He had exited Home Hardware with a large box under his arm, but stopped to talk to a bent-over man in plaid shirt and overalls.

A sudden impulse to boot the fenders and smash the headlights of the red truck seized Adam. But he stopped himself. Mark did not welcome or want his anger. He had attached himself to Doug, in ways Adam could never understand.

He kept walking, down the street to his office.

Across the province, the flood waters had all subsided.

At Adam's cabin, the river ice and soil on the banks had thawed enough to allow his waterline to pull freely. On the previous morning, the plumber had checked the lines for leaks and primed the pump.

As Adam shaved, he studied his face in the mirror. Since early February, he had only used this bathroom a couple of times a day, preferring to wait until he got to work or until he went to Mike's farmhouse for a shower. After he finished scraping off the lather and whiskers, he pushed his cheeks back and forth, yanked at the skin under his eyes. He stared at the pink membranes and the fine wrinkles. He thought he looked pale and old, more tired and unhealthy than he remembered.

At that moment, Adam did not like himself.

# Death Do Us Part

It was the only road back to town.

Slowly, ever so slowly, Kelly Klassen drove the agency sedan, a five-year-old Ford Taurus, over the loose gravel. The washboard wobbled her gut and she regretted the tuna sandwich and large bottle of Coke that she had devoured for lunch. She could not rush, but felt pressured to hurry. The unfinished reports sitting on her desk reminded her of land mines. Thick files lay untouched, sometime for months, until they blew up in her face. She could rarely predict why, or when.

It was August; her holidays started in two weeks. In most professional jobs, summer means a slower pace. But not for social workers who specialize in child protection. Every co-worker Kelly could name was swamped. Tempers flared when kids were home from school; their presence interfered with the all-night parties spilling out of overheated houses.

This was her first full-time job after graduating from social work, but she already knew too well the paradox of her chosen career. Child protection workers balance on a tightrope of flip-flopping public opinion. On one day, the media target them for being heartless and autocratic when they removed children from a home. On another day, in a similar situation, they get pilloried for not yanking kids out of dangerous environments. This contradiction made everyone in Child and Family Services stressed, jumpy, and hesitant to make decisions.

The one constant in her job was the volume — an endless, pounding waterfall of expectations. Every weekday, and sometimes when she was on call on Saturday and Sunday, a new family crisis erupted, and she'd jump in her car to drive out and investigate. The bigwigs in charge didn't seem to care much for the actual humans involved. Instead, they asked for more reports, more accountability, and more obedience to convoluted and complicated ass-covering procedures.

How often had she burned with shame, talking to bewildered mothers? Just yesterday, she had droned on and on, explaining department policy, to Betty Redmoon, a twenty-year-old with two kids, who could not keep her meth-addicted boyfriend away from her isolated cabin. And how often had she actually feared for her own physical safety? The week before, she had to ask a Mountie to accompany her to a falling-down house trailer, after she got a call about a psychotic mother who had been drunk for a week and was starving her three kids and tying them up and burning them with lit cigarettes. Her middle-class optimism could not shield her soul from the grim troika of poverty, intoxicants, and abuse she faced every day.

She shook her head to clear the visions of recent conflicts, straightened her shoulders, and smoothed her hair behind her ears. The overloaded desk would have to wait. This road demanded her concentration. Its repeated loops around the swamps, lakes, and rock cuts of the Precambrian Shield made the trip back to town last over an hour. Raised in the small prairie city of Steinbach, with four years at university on the flatlands of Winnipeg, she was unaccustomed to such winding, hilly, and uninhabited roads.

It had not rained in two weeks. In the distance, the gravel road shimmered, scorched and wavering, in a haze of refracted light. She swallowed hard and ran her tongue along the fissures of her lips; grey particles had settled on her teeth and throat.

By the Loon Lake railway intersection, she approached a rare straight stretch. She could speed up here, but could not relax. Although she drove this road at least once a week and had never seen any moose on this section, she had to watch. Her boss had told her how the lumbering animals liked to cross here, moving east from Loon Lake to feed in the marsh. He also told her about the seventeen-year-old boy from the nearby reserve who had smashed head-on into a bull moose one sunny summer morning and ended up in a wheel chair. She did not know the young man, but thought about him every time she drove this piece of road. Torn between her fear of collision and her compulsion to get back to her office, she accelerated.

Then she saw a flicker of movement on the rise up ahead.

She braked. Two forms emerged from a cluster of spruce trees, near the railway tracks. Squinting into the haze, she made out a couple, walking slowly, heads down, both of them dressed in jeans and dark, long-sleeved shirts. The man held the woman by the arm as he led her toward the opening where the tracks lay. Kelly knew that locals sometimes flagged down the train to catch rides into town, even though it passed by only once a day. She drove closer and noticed the man dragged a bulky blue bag, the type used to carry hockey equipment. From the way they moved, both looked exhausted and over-heated from the afternoon sun.

The couple halted. A small puff of dust rose up where the man plopped the bag down in the gravel at the side of the road. Kelly did not want to stop. She wanted to return to her office as soon as possible, to work some overtime. Besides, unauthorized passengers were not allowed in agency cars.

She blinked to clear her eyes. Then she realized she knew the middle-aged couple. They lived at Crooked Lake, the place she had just left. On two occasions, she had met Frank and Anna Sinclair but hadn't dealt with them as clients. Both times, they were inebriated and had greeted her with laughs and shouts.

She couldn't remember exactly what they had said to her, but it stuck in her mind that their comments went something along the lines of "Hello, city girl, how are you? Do you like our reserve? Did you come here to go fishing?" She had smiled at them, unsure if these salutations were jokes or insults. As far as she knew, they had not caused any major trouble in their lakeside community and were not involved in any of her co-workers' files.

Kelly reduced her speed. Her car was barely moving when she got closer to the couple.

Frank looked up and waved his hands to clear the clouds of dust, or maybe chase away deer-flies, and nodded at her. Anna did not look up, only leaned further into his shoulder.

Kelly stopped and rolled down the window. "Are you headed into town?"

An absurd question, she realized, before she finished it.

"Yeah, we wanted to catch the train," Frank said.

Kelly could not detect a whiff of sarcasm. Or alcohol. "When does it come?"

"In another two hours."

She could justify picking them up if she claimed they were current clients. Besides, it was far away from human habitation, in thirty degree heat. Anna wilted as she slumped against the car.

"I can give you a ride."

"Good, we need to see a doctor," the man stated.

Kelly could not detect any urgency. "A doctor?"

"Yeah, my wife, Anna, is not too well."

At the mention of her name, his wife lifted her head. A few gaps from missing teeth showed when she smiled and then winced. Underneath the brown tones, her skin looked pasty and dull, as if encased in drying cement. Her pallor convinced Kelly. They needed a ride.

"I can take you to the hospital. The doctor's office will be closed."

"Okay . . . good." Frank said these two words as if he lost interest in between them.

He swung the door wide and manoeuvred Anna into the

back seat. She settled in with a grunt, while Kelly quickly closed the driver's side window, hoping to preserve as much coolness as possible from the sedan's overworked air conditioner. Although she expected she might learn more as they wound along the road, Frank did not speak for the next few minutes.

Whenever she could spare her attention from the curves, Kelly checked the couple in her rear view mirror. Anna sat with head down, eyes closed, leaning against Frank's left shoulder. On the corners, he reached out his right arm to support her.

After a series of bone-jarring jolts, Kelly glanced up to check again. To her surprise, Frank looked at her, wet his lips, and spoke softly, "Are you the social worker?"

"Yes."

"I seen you before."

"I come out once a week."

"You took Billy and Karen's kids last month."

For a moment, she considered the dangers of engaging in this topic. In her short career, she had apprehended six children from three families at Crooked Lake. Could her passengers be the grandparents of any of these children? Despite washboards and washouts, she risked quick, but regular, glances in the rear-view mirror. Frank's pockmarked features revealed no emotion.

Convinced she could not detect any hostility, Kelly gave her full attention to the road. She wanted to know what "not too well," meant, but something stopped her from asking.

Every few minutes, Anna moaned. The woman did not smell of alcohol, but she could not sit upright, swaying in and out along the edges of Kelly's sight-lines. For a brief second, she glimpsed Anna's eyes through a thick tangle of dark hair.

Despite the grinding air conditioner, the sedan's interior grew closer, hotter, almost chewable. After another fifteen minutes, the road straightened out so Kelly sped up. When the car swung and slid on the corners, Anna moaned louder.

"Sorry, but I need to get back to work," Kelly mumbled.

Her eyes watered from staring at the road, her head ached, and her tongue felt like a piece of birch bark. She alternated between watching the road and glancing in the mirror, in hopes her passengers might initiate even a superficial conversation. Had cultural differences created this silence? Or did they hate the "system" she represented?

"She doesn't seem to be feeling too well," Kelly ventured, paraphrasing Frank's earlier words.

"No."

"Is she sick?"

"No."

She flinched, determined to continue, despite the one-word responses. She considered, then resisted, questioning their state of intoxication.

"Is she . . . hurt?"

"Oh, yeah. She's hurt."

Encouraged by the extra words, she asked, "What's wrong?"

After this question, the conversation halted.

Kelly watched the thistles along the edge of the road and thought about the stilted dialogue. These downy heads matched her tenuous interaction with her passengers, so easily blown away by sudden gusts.

Frank stared out the window. A long moment passed before he spoke.

"She is bleeding."

Kelly inhaled and exhaled twice, long and deep. His revelation, hard-won, almost skittish, was too important to let slip away. Careful, conscious that she was now grilling him, she asked, "What happened?"

Another long moment slid past.

Once more, she glimpsed Frank's right arm encircling Anna's shoulder to steady her. He swallowed hard and pushed his free hand through his hair.

"I shot her. We were fighting."

Kelly blinked and her mouth fell open. Then she pressed her palm hard against the right side of her forehead. She wanted to push this image out of her head. She stared at the mirror and tried to peek over the seat, to check if he had concealed the gun in the hockey bag. The zipper was broken and the bag now gaped open on the seat beside Anna. All Kelly could see was some rumpled clothing — dirty laundry, maybe.

The car fish-tailed toward a large pond. She braked and yanked the steering wheel sideways. Anna groaned. Swirls of dust enveloped the car as it skidded to a stop, its front wheels resting next to a clump of cattails.

Kelly backed the sedan onto the middle of the road, her shoulders shaking in relief — and disbelief.

Oblivious to their near-accident, Frank continued in his monotone. "Yeah, I was pissed at her. I used my shotgun. She was pretty far away, standing by the clothes line. I just wanted to scare her. I didn't think it would hit her. She has a bunch of buckshot holes in her back."

Kelly started to drive again, slowly. She wanted to turn around and face him, but she needed to get Anna to the hospital as quickly as possible. Fumbling with her right foot, she pressed harder on the gas pedal. She looked in the mirror again and saw a bead of moisture trickle down Frank's left cheek, cleaving a shadowy trail from forehead to jaw bone. He seemed mesmerized by the passing trees.

Again, she ended up watching him too long. The car lurched into a pot hole; Anna slumped sideways. Before he pulled her upright, Kelly looked back again. A patch of blood had spread across the beige fabric of the back seat.

She pulled her eyes away. If she didn't pay attention to the road, they'd slide off and it might be hours before another vehicle came along. If they dropped into one of the deeper ditches, other drivers might not even notice them. And, if it was filled with water, they could drown.

She forced herself to refocus and checked her watch. Another fifteen minutes to town. Anna yelped when the car bounced over a rock. Frank did not respond; he just pulled her close and held her there. A thin line of drool appeared at the side of her mouth as she panted in short, sharp bursts.

Finally, Kelly reached the pavement. Although the hospital was now only ten minutes away, the highway curved around several more lakes and rock cuts so the maximum speed was restricted. She pulled away from the stop sign and floored it. The tires squealed, the engine roared, and, within a few seconds, the car sped up to twice the posted limit. She prayed some zealous cop would stop her. She wanted someone else to take responsibility for the bleeding woman.

Closer to town, the highway straightened and leveled. Focused on the rising speedometer, she rounded a wide curve and drove right past the hospital entrance. She swore, slowed to twenty and then stopped. Frank's forearms banged against the back of her seat.

Kelly spun the car around and raced back to the approach to the hospital. At the emergency entrance, she turned off the engine and looked at her passengers. Frank opened his door and attempted to haul Anna out of the rear seat.

Kelly shouted, "No, no! I'll get help!"

He grunted and stopped pulling on his wife.

Kelly sprinted from the agency car to the emergency entrance. She wondered if he might run away, but she could not worry about him.

The glass panels slid open. She ran down the short hallway to the reception desk and yelled, "I've got a woman with a gunshot wound! I don't know how long it's been. She looks bad."

The woman at the desk responded immediately. Three attendants appeared and raced toward the car. They lifted Anna out of the back seat, strapped her onto a gurney, swaddled her in a blanket, and rushed her up the entrance ramp. The sliding doors swished open. Propelled by a growing entourage of attendants, the gurney clattered down the hallway and then disappeared.

Kelly returned to her car, opened the back door and stood, transfixed by the bloodstain. Frank still sat on the left, leaning against the front seat, his face buried in his forearms. His posture surprised Kelly; it was his first show of emotion.

A nurse appeared at her side, asking for details. Kelly turned and responded, spitting out answers without thinking about words.

In about five or ten minutes, an RCMP cruiser drove up, lights flashing, no siren, and two officers dragged Frank out of the agency car. They handcuffed him and put him in the back seat of the cruiser. One of the officers, a young, redheaded constable, asked Kelly a few questions and gave her his card, and then they drove away.

Kelly watched them as they moved down the hill.

Her head began to throb. Her bones and tissues felt rubbery and useless. Explanations, cleanups, reports, could wait until tomorrow.

THE NEXT MORNING, Kelly drove a different agency car up the winding entrance to the hospital. Although she did not know why, she wanted to see Anna, to hear her voice. The nurse on duty showed her into a dim room, smelling of floor polish and antiseptic, curtains halfway drawn. A long lump lay under pristine sheets. Faraway televisions echoed in the corridor. Kelly sat on the vinyl chair and waited.

After ten minutes, Anna stirred. She groaned and coughed, dragged herself into an upright position, clutching her left side.

Kelly spoke, almost in a whisper. "You may not remember me, but my name is Kelly Klassen. I'm the social worker for Crooked Lake. I drove you here yesterday."

Anna pulled her body higher in the bed, wiped her hand across her lips, and looked Kelly in the eye. She asked, "Where's Frank? They don't tell me nothin' here. They don't want to upset me. Well, I'm plenty upset. I want to go home."

Anna reached out to grasp Kelly's left forearm.

"I think he's still in jail." Kelly did not withdraw her arm.

"Why?"

"The police wanted to keep him there. So he doesn't hurt you again."

"Why can't he come get me right now?"

Kelly did not know the answer, but knew she didn't want Anna to get up off the bed.

"Why do you need to see him?"

Anna leaned forward and dug her fingers even deeper into Kelly's arm.

"He has to take me . . . home."

Kelly extricated her skin from Anna's fist, finger by finger. She stroked her burning forearm with her opposite hand.

She stared hard at Anna, as if seeing her for the first time.

# Breaking Through

ANNETTE WOKE WITH A JERK OF HER HEAD. THE CLOCK READ 8:45 a.m. Her alarm blinked but did not buzz. She assumed she had overslept; then she remembered it was Saturday. Missing work remained a recurring phobia for her, even after twenty-five years of teaching.

Because her bay window faced the rising sun, her bedroom was already filled with light. A few metres away from the cedar deck, the Winnipeg River flowed past her home. The river's beauty changed according to season and weather. She often imagined the scene outside her window was recreated daily to surprise and delight only her.

Today, in early December, she stared across the water. In front of her house, the opposite wooded shore lay about two hundred metres to the east. Poplar and spruce grew to the water's edge, interspersed by small plots of farmland cut out of the wilderness and now abandoned.

Annette lived in a two-bedroom bungalow in the village of St. Hilaire. This small francophone community, situated on the edge of the boreal forest, was mostly occupied by retired pulp cutters, paper makers, mill workers, and their families. Because of the recent shutdown and demolition of the paper mill, several houses in St. Hilaire had sat empty for months.

The river moved, rippling and bright, caught halfway in the midst of winter freeze-up. Each day, the flexible white sheets had advanced further into the center. Uneven curls of ice grew from the shores.

The steel-gray surface of the river disguised the volume of flow. Some parts never froze completely, even in the grip of minus thirty, such was the quickness of the water. But that was upstream, not in her view. The wider areas downstream could almost be called a lake and always froze first.

The ice's jagged edges sparkled in the strengthening light. If the weather stayed cold, the expanding sheets would join up in less than a week. Jets of mist spiraled from the surface, as if the water were fighting against the release of stored August heat.

The river quickened her senses; she had never seen it so beautiful. Then she remembered all the other days. After another minute of contemplation, she rolled over to the edge of the mattress, forced herself to stand and walked stiffly into the kitchen to make coffee. Because this Saturday stretched long and vacant before her, she decided to stay in bed a bit longer. Besides, she wanted to savour the scene framed by her bedroom window, before it evaporated beneath the rising sun.

Not many people she knew allowed themselves such simple pleasures. Like watching river ice inch toward union. Like eating toast and jam in bed. Like reading until she fell asleep again, no matter what time it was. Like drinking as much coffee as possible without getting up to pee.

After the coffee brewed, and toast browned, she returned, with loaded tray, to her king size bed. With a 600-page murder mystery tucked under her arm, she slid between the sheets and flopped back against the pillows. On mornings like this, she relished living alone, with no obligations. The daily drudgery of a grade six teacher's life faded into the sidelines of her mind. After she rejected the idea of more toast, she reached down to rub her knees. This was the other reason she preferred to stay in bed. As she kneaded the joints, she thought about her lifelong cycle of pain and gain. At times, her arthritis caused her to become less active. Less activity caused her weight to increase. Now in her early fifties, she had accepted her limited mobility. Whether by circumstance or inclination, she cherished her more contemplative existence. She ate the last of the toast and flicked the crumbs onto her carpet. Then she snuggled under the sky blue duvet and started the next chapter.

ONE HOUR AND THIRTY MINUTES LATER, the bedside phone rang. Her head had slumped forward in response to the book's stalled momentum and her glasses had fallen off. After she groped around for the phone receiver, she answered in a woolly-minded mumble. She imagined that she could not hear as well as usual.

"Hello, good morning, *bonjour.*" She patted the hills and valleys of the duvet in search of her fallen spectacles. She had broken three pairs the same way.

The voice on the other end started slowly, and continued slowly. It sounded as hollow and strained as a diesel engine on a winter morning.

"Annette … I'm so glad to find you at home."

She could not recognize the clenched tones. One of her sisters, maybe, but she could not tell which one.

"Are you all right?" Annette asked, softly, and sat up straight against her pillows. She spotted, and retrieved, her glasses perched on the outermost edge of the duvet.

"Yes. I wanted to tell you. Before you heard it on the radio. Or on television."

The stumbling voice had her full attention. She flipped her long dark braid over her shoulder, leaned forward, as if urging the speaker forward, like a rider encouraging a tired horse.

"It's Uncle Anton. He was skating. On the lake at St. Francis Park." The speaker gulped hard before continuing. "You know, the one they made with the new dam."

Finally, Annette recognized the broken voice. It was her oldest sister, Maria, who worked night shifts at the hospital and usually slept in on Saturday mornings. Annette wanted to make sense of the call, but in her newly aroused muddle, she could not understand why Maria wanted to talk about their energetic uncle and a duck pond. She grabbed the end of her braid and combed her fingers repeatedly through the tuft of hair at its end.

Maria was now crying, but kept talking. Her voice accelerated, propelled by the tears toward the conclusion. "This morning, the ice was fine, at least six inches, where he started. He even cut a hole. Lots of other people were out on it. At least twenty. He loved to skate on that little lake. But he was only in his sixties. He loved to get outside and exercise. Especially in the winter. Everybody thought it was thick enough. They don't know what happened."

Maria's voice slowed again. "They just found a big hole. It's as if . . . "

"*Attend, une minute.* Are you telling me he fell through the ice?"

Annette realized Maria was creeping close to hysteria. Her sister's words had rushed and spilled out so rapidly, Annette wanted to snatch her back to a more level place, to rein in her terror.

Maria's single word reply dropped like a brick in a pail of water.

"Yes."

"And they have not found any sign of him. Yet."

"Yes."

Another brick.

"What time did this happen?"

"Around ten o'clock."

A heavy tumble of impacts. The tears began to spill. Maria was now sobbing.

Annette glanced at her clock radio. It read 11:36 a.m. She picked up a pad and pen from her night table. She wrote down details. They seemed strangely important right now. Or maybe it was the teacher in her, using an automatic strategy to regain control in a crisis. She noticed her hands shook as she wrote, but she pried more information from her sister. The RCMP had already arrived at the park, they expected the divers at any minute, and they had begun to notify family.

Annette's teeth ground when the jarring cliché slid from her mouth. "The only thing we can do now is wait."

Maria was not reassured. Several times, Annette tried variations of the same theme. Then she attempted a different tactic. After a few minutes, she had almost persuaded Maria, and herself, that their uncle had climbed out of the water, behind some trees, without anyone noticing. He was back at his mobile home, wrapped in a blanket, curled up on his leather couch, drinking tea, laughing and chatting with his cats.

After Maria hung up, Annette could not sit in her bed any longer. She rushed into the kitchen but realized she had nowhere to go and not much to do. She rinsed out the coffee carafe and wiped up the crumbs.

Despite Maria's outburst, Annette knew her sister would want to keep occupied, and grounded, by telling and retelling. Maria had offered to take care of spreading the grim news. So that meant Annette did not need to phone anyone.

She thought about distracting herself with the murder mystery abandoned on her duvet, but the gory murders now repulsed her. She paced and watched the phone, for twenty minutes, until her knees began to twinge in protest. The oversized recliner in her living room seemed like a compromise. She would not be lying in bed, which felt disloyal and lax during this crucial interlude. But she could rest her legs. And continue to stare at the phone.

It also seemed reasonable to phone some friends. She called one person, but it upset her so much she stopped. The only thing to do now was wait. She hated that stupid cliché.

THIRTY MINUTES LATER, a flash of motion in her peripheral vision caught her attention. A moving object bounded forward into the middle of her view. Curious, she flipped up out of the recliner and rose to her feet. When she approached the living room window, the dark thing assumed an identity. In the strip of open water closest to the shore, a white-tail deer, with six-point antlers, splashed frantically to pull itself back onto solid ice.

Annette blinked, rubbed her eyes, shook her head. She stood transfixed, as if witnessing a car wreck. It looked too surreal, too bizarre, too coincidental to be actually happening.

Again and again, the animal crashed into the edges of the ice and shattered them with the force of its propulsion. After what seemed like an hour to Annette, the deer stopped battling and paddled quietly, just to stay afloat. Then it rested its head on the battered ice. She could see its rib cage heave in and out, back and forth. The tortured gasping reminded her of an incident in her class when a student suffered an asthma attack. They had called the ambulance.

She stared and struggled to control her own breathing. On a normal day, the deer's plight would have aroused her sympathies but the unreality of the two connected events completely overwhelmed her senses. She could not breathe; she could not think. As if she herself had herself been plunged headfirst into frigid waters — immobilized, paralyzed, frozen by panic.

She wanted to go outside to check on the deer, but felt nailed to the floor. Her heart thumped so loudly and powerfully, she crossed her arms over her sternum, to prevent it from breaking loose inside her rib cage.

With a gasp, she collapsed back into the recliner. After a few panting breaths, she tried to hoist herself up. It felt as if a giant hand pushed down on her chest. Annette succumbed to the squeezing terror, let her body go limp. She breathed deeply for a few seconds and then hurled herself out of the chair.

Once upright, she realized she had no idea what to do next. She could not call on her neighbours for help. The ones who hadn't left for Texas or Mexico were gone for the day, caught up in the rush of pre-Christmas shopping. She narrowed her eyes, considered the option of venturing onto the ice, and then admitted to herself it was not only impractical, but ridiculous, even if she weighed much less. The stag was stronger and heavier than any human, with horns designed by nature to be weapons. Also, it thrashed around in its death struggle, fueled by adrenaline.

Her mouth suddenly felt dry and toxic. She rushed to the kitchen sink and bent over it, to spit and cough, spit and cough. Her abdomen lurched but she did not vomit. She stood up, turned on the tap, let the water run over her fingers. When they began to ache from the cold, she shivered, thinking about her uncle and how he must have panicked when his body shut down and his arms and legs stopped working. She spat once more to clear her mouth and drank two glasses of water.

When the shaking slowed, she turned to her hall closet, beside the back door. She dressed in parka and snow pants and then thrust her feet into leather Sorrels. She did not usually wear such heavy winter clothes. But she had them and she wanted to protect herself. She clomped across the living room, slid open the patio door, and stepped out into the mists flying off the river.

She crunched down the steps from her deck and through the skiffs of re-frozen snow. Trudging through the stiff grass of the shared lawn, she struggled to assemble her thoughts and emotions into a manageable order. How long could a deer last, the way it was exerting itself? She thought of its terror and could not help but remember her uncle. She squeezed hard on both sides of her temples with mitten-clad hands, and almost knocked off her woolen hat. She did not want that graphic picture burned into her brain.

When she reached the edge of the river, she peered at the water sliding past. It looked like molten pewter, opaque, gray, and glowing from reflected light. The ice appeared to be less than twenty centimetres thick, judging from what she could see from the shore. The stag splashed more violently when she approached, but stopped when she spoke.

"What the hell are you doing in there?"

The animal swung its rack around, to sniff and stare. The large, brown eyes, usually so appealing, conveyed a new emotion. They held a glassy, bloated deadness.

She locked eyes with the animal. *"Don't you know better? It's too thin!"*

Her voice echoed from the opposite bank, bouncing easily in the chilled air. The deer stared at the human for a full fifteen seconds. Annette imagined pleas for mercy, nets, a boat, a rifle. Then she screamed, *"Couldn't you wait?"*

More echoes.

She screeched louder. *"Now you're going to die, and I can't save you!"*

After this last outburst, the deer stopped watching her and resumed its battle with the ice. It snorted in sharp breaths, threw its wide torso forward and upward, achieving nothing, except more smashed ice. More scraped-off pieces of hide. Tufts of coarse hair, and streaks of blood, were scattered at intervals along the edges.

After a few minutes, the deer paused. Annette watched the animal repeat this cycle six times, with each scramble getting shorter, and each pause growing longer.

She stood motionless. She felt compelled to assist, but no ideas came to her. The deer would die soon, either of hypothermia, heart failure, or drowning. It could not crash around much longer.

The stag's muzzle bled from a wide gash. It thrust its body much lower out of the water now. Its breaths sounded impossibly rapid, and raspy, in the cool air. A light breeze had come up, blowing the mist sideways. At times, the deer disappeared from her sight.

Then she thought of an action. Not necessarily a solution, but an action. She turned away as quickly as the footing would allow and limped back to her condominium. Her knees felt like mill stones grinding together. The cold air had nearly seized her joints.

When she entered the warmth, through the patio doors, a wave of anxiety almost knocked her flat on the floor. She removed her outerwear, staggered to her recliner, and collapsed.

Once a sense of equilibrium returned, she flipped open the phone book beside her chair. She found the number of the conservation office. It calmed her to believe someone, somewhere, could help. She could rouse assistance, despite her pounding pulse and racing thoughts.

The phone rang and rang. Then she remembered. "Of course, it's Saturday. No one will be there."

Once again fighting for normal breathing, she willed herself to concentrate. Her brain had stalled, flooded by the joined images of human and deer thrashing in the water.

"Stop. Think. Think. Alice works at school. Her husband is a conservation officer. I know her number. I can call him at home." She said each of these words slowly and carefully, to reassure herself her mind still functioned.

While she waited for the phone to be picked up, she doubted the seriousness of her request. Deer, and lots of other animals, probably drowned this way all the time.

When a man finally answered, her words came in a rush. "Hello, Martin. This is Annette Duval. Sorry to bother you at home, but this is an emergency. A deer is in the river in front of my place."

Emergency. Yes, an emergency. She could scarcely believe the quick but level sounds coming out of her head. As she explained, she unraveled her braid and ran her fingers through the long curls. She wanted the man to come immediately. She doubted if she had enough energy to finish the conversation, but conquered her urge to stop, hang up, cry, several times during the call.

"The deer broke through the ice. Now it's stuck in the water."

SHE DESPISED THE BANAL EXCHANGE OF DETAILS. With a surge of energy, she described location, time in water, size of animal.

Martin asked brief, practical questions, and, finally, "Are you certain he's still alive?"

Annette wound and unwound the cord of her phone. Wound and unwound strands of hair. For an instant, she became so bewildered, she could not remember which situation she wanted to discuss, the deer or her uncle. The two had fused together. She shook out her hair with her fingers, blinked to stop the tears, and sucked in her breath.

Carefully, thoroughly, she answered the rest of his questions. When she thought of how the officer might react if she bawled, she could feel herself sliding toward a fit of giggles. It was only a deer, after all. She breathed in deeply several times, to shore up her imploding composure. Martin hesitated for a few seconds, and then spoke in a low, calm voice. "There's really not much we can do. It's best to let nature take its course. Whatever is going to happen will happen."

"But, what about . . . " Annette interrupted him and then halted. He might wonder why she sounded so agitated.

He repeated his last statement.

"You mean there is absolutely nothing. . . ." She interrupted again and stopped again. Suddenly, it felt as if someone had poured warm massage oil over her shoulders and kneaded it into her vibrating muscles. Her tight neck uncoiled its tendons. The flood of relief surprised her. It was only a deer, after all.

Martin said, "If the buck is going to die, he will. It's a part of nature. But he might also get out of the water."

She thanked him and said good-bye.

His placid voice was exactly what she needed. She sat beside the phone for another thirty minutes, stared at it, as if she had to memorize the numbers and letters for a test. It did not ring.

She finally got up and looked out at the river. The milky sun, now high in an overcast sky, played hide and seek with scudding clouds. The deer was gone.

At first, she thought the current must have sucked it under the ice. Then she saw an indentation in the snow, on the ice, closer to the other side of the river — where a large body could have dragged itself up and across. She squinted to penetrate the dancing mist and decided to believe she saw faint imprints of tracks leading toward the opposite shore.

She did not know exactly why or how, but she felt ready to face the phone call. She wrapped herself in a knitted blanket and waited in her recliner.

The call did not come until later that night.

# Dead Skunk

LENA KNEW IT WAS GOING TO BE DIFFICULT WHEN THEY WOULD not leave the skunk alone. It lay near the perimeter of the open field, wedged between the furrows. A length of braided blue and white baling twine wound around the neck of the bloated carcass. They resembled surgeons in an operating theatre, seven children huddled around the inert animal.

One of the older boys, Franklin, grabbed the twine and began to drag the corpse, running through the ridges of the ploughed field, stirring up skiffs of black dust. Like a drunken water skier, the skunk's head bounced off bumps in the soil. The rest of the children fell in behind Franklin. They followed him across the field, whooping and laughing as if it were a parade.

"You need to leave that thing alone!" Lena shouted into the wind.

They did not look back or speak, but continued racing after Franklin and his bizarre pull-toy.

"It stinks! How can you even stand to be near it?" she shouted even louder.

They did not respond. The bouncing skunk and the running children were now silhouetted in the afternoon sun, almost hidden in a blur of dust. She put her hand to her forehead to shield her eyes from the glare and then pushed unruly strands away from her face.

"What the. . . ." This mild profanity bubbled to her lips, and almost slid out, but she restrained the impulse to swear. After all, she was the teacher here, and they were Hutterites.

"Let go of that dead thing! You might get some of the smell on you! I don't want that stench in the school!" She directed these commands at Franklin, but he had his head up and his legs churning, a small mule with the bit in his teeth. He obviously had no intention of stopping.

"You need to wait right there!"

None of the children halted. They continued hooting and running. All of them were too captivated by the white-striped corpse bumping along behind Franklin.

Besides, now they were too far away. The brisk northerly breeze made it impossible for her words to have much effect anyway. The sounds got swallowed by swirling gusts. All the wind did was waft the scent of the skunk's remains up her nostrils. She was not convinced they would listen to her even if they could hear her. She wanted to stick to her lesson plan so it seemed she had no other choice but to chase them down.

They had a hundred-metre head start and the footing was uneven.

Lena was thirty-five years old and considered it highly undignified to be stumbling through a freshly ploughed field on her first day of class. She was supposed to be teaching an art lesson. But she figured she could outrun them, if only on the merits of her longer legs. She sprinted across the shifting ridges, wondering why anyone would choose to play with such a stinking mess. She also wondered why she was huffing and puffing across a twenty-acre field on the border of the Pine Grove Hutterite colony, in eastern Manitoba, pursuing these apparently hearing-impaired children. Two days earlier, she did not even know they existed.

Although she had lived only twenty kilometres from the colony for seven years, since her move to the area after her marriage, she had never visited it. To her great surprise, in the second week of September, the principal of the school, Jakob Hofer, had phoned to ask if she'd be interested in teaching two days a week on a temporary contract. He said she could try it out to see if she liked it and the agreement could be reviewed at the end of three months. Several questions had zipped around in her head as he spoke. *Don't Hutterites want their kids taught by their own colony-raised and super-obedient members, usually young women who don't plan to get married? Does he know I'm a hard-core feminist and might not fit with their fifteenth-century patriarchal traditions? Does he know coffee shop pundits are now talking about me?*

Jakob had asked her to work with the youngest class in the school, a multi-level combination of grades one to four. Adam, Hansel, and Emily were in grade four. Franklin and Simon were in grade three. Although Franklin was supposed to be in grade four, he had been kept back. Abraham was Franklin's youngest brother and the only one in grade two. The youngest child in the school was Jeremiah, in grade one.

Although it was unusual to be hired in September, Lena had eagerly accepted a chance for an interview. On the long weekend in August, her husband's brother had appeared at her door with a large envelope. Her husband, Timothy Havak, did not want to be married anymore, so he went fishing and sent his older brother to inform her and serve her with the necessary documents.

The arrival of the divorce papers meant not only the end of her seven-year marriage, but also the end of her job. She had been employed in his accounting business. She read the served documents and concluded that he was collaborating with the local lawyers on a book called *How to Dump a Wife While Scaring the Hell out of Her.*

Lena jogged through the dusty furrows and thought about the phone conversation she had had with her friend, Jenny Austin, on the night before she took this teaching job. She had been complaining about how hard it was to find an unsullied lawyer, one who was not already connected to Tim.

Jenny replied, "Speaking of lawyers, the other day I met one who whined to me, 'Why do these people instantly dislike me, when they find out I'm a lawyer?' "

Lena waited, without comment.

Jenny laughed for half a minute before she gave the punch line.

"It just saves time!"

Lena ran faster, smiling as she envisioned Jenny's hoots of amusement. Soon the memory of her friend's laughter fused with the eerily similar yelps of her stampeding students. Sweating and panting, she approached the cluster of children, who had slowed to a halt. She did not expect to catch up with them so quickly, but it appeared that the head of the skunk was almost severed. Lena guessed they wanted to savour the moment of decapitation. They stopped and turned when she jogged up to them.

"Didn't you hear me? I asked you to wait."

She paused to catch her breath, and, once again, push her hair out of her face. Seven pairs of eyes swung up from the carcass to stare innocently at her. Then the eyes dropped down, in the direction of the skunk.

"You might get that smelly musk on you. Do you usually play with dead animals?"

No one answered. Lena reminded herself that English was not their first language. She repeated the question, more slowly this time.

Wiry, dark-haired Franklin, puller of the skunk, squinted into the sun, and spat a fast stream of phlegm into the dirt. It landed directly beside the corpse. A puff of dust rose as he yanked at the string. "Yo, we kill chickens. By the hundreds. Big Jim shot this skunk and dragged it here. I want to see it close."

Lena could not follow the logic, but was relieved to know they could understand her. She could not fathom why a dead skunk would be deposited on a ploughed field; Franklin's explanation made as much sense as anything else.

She knew it was irrational, but she could not get the idea out of her head that they had somehow caught and killed the animal while she had been preoccupied listening to young Jeremiah. He had given her a lengthy description of his grandmother's infected, ingrown toenail. Because of the slurred English, accented by Low German, she needed to listen carefully. When Jeremiah slid his grimy, and warty, hand into hers, he grinned up at her. Lena nodded politely when she considered it appropriate. He continued to smile through the whole explanation. Even when he told Lena the toe had to be amputated. Or at least she thought that was what he said. Because of this one-sided conversation with Jeremiah, she had not been paying attention to the other six students as they had wandered across the field and discovered the rotten skunk.

"Let go of the string, Franklin. The skunk needs to be left where it is." Her voice was more forceful, now that she had recovered her breath.

Lena hoped it would not nauseate the field workers too much if they shredded the rotted remains of the skunk in a swather at a later date, but she really did not want to tell Franklin to drag it back to where he found it. She suspected another impromptu, and riotous, parade would erupt. Franklin pitched the length of twine at the skunk's bloated anus. As he spun on his heel, the rest of the children watched him. Franklin seemed poised to bolt back to the school.

"Wait a minute! Who remembers why we came outside today?" Lena's tone was bright, exasperated. She wondered if they could detect the mild desperation.

"I know. We are going to draw. I love to draw!" Emily lifted her hands upward and clapped in excitement. Sunny lasers of joy radiated from her broad, beaming features.

Lena was taken aback by the sudden enthusiasm. She looked at the group, now lined up and facing her. She smiled at Emily, who was very blonde, and bigger than all the boys.

"Right! And who remembers why we were coming outside

to draw? Why are we going over there to the 'under-land,' as you call it?" Lena pointed north, emphasizing every syllable, but she still could not be sure how much English they understood. She gestured at Hansel for an answer.

Hansel also had straw-coloured hair and sky-blue eyes, and he was almost as tall as Emily, but wider. He grinned at Lena with a daunting array of white teeth, a miniature Nordic shark. "We are going to draw something in nature. A scene we seen many times."

Then he paused. "A scene we seen! Ha! Ha! Ha!"

His loud repetition of these English homophones provoked a round of mimicking laughter. The youngest ones, Jeremiah and Abraham, dropped onto the ground, as if felled by waves of mania. Lena grabbed their blackened hands and hoisted them both to their feet, and smiled — but only with her mouth, not her eyes. *How had Hutterite children ever gained a reputation as being shy and compliant?* She decided these children were ruckus-contagious, primed for almost any excuse to explode with merriment.

"That's right, Hansel. We are going to choose something familiar. A tree, a rock, a plant. And we are going to look at it carefully. We have pencils, erasers, clipboards. So we can sit and look. And draw it as we really see it. Not as we think we remember it. Does everyone understand?"

Emily, and Adam, the other boy in grade four, nodded gravely. The other children scraped mud off their scuffed sneakers, chuckled into their hands, and then glanced sideways at each other. Lena stopped talking and glared at them, with her sternest teacher-face.

She spoke louder. "I want you to pick one thing, something simple, and *really* look at it. Once you have looked at it carefully, for at least three minutes, then you can start drawing. Do you all understand? "

The five students who had been snorting into their fists bowed their heads forward and stood still. Lena waited for a response.

After a few seconds of silence, she shook her head, rolled her eyes and thumped her forehead with the palm of her hand. Even after this rattling smack, she could not understand why she needed to keep repeating instructions. It was not clear to her if it was a language barrier or garden-variety passive defiance.

Maybe the assignment was not suited to such young children. Or maybe the novelty of the wide blue sky, the open air, and the liberation from desks was too stimulating. It might have been much easier to stay in the classroom. Also, she remembered, art was not a part of any of their recent school experiences. Not until Jakob, the principal, had decided he wanted her to work part-time. He seemed especially interested in her skills in art, physical education, and music, because the children had never been taught any of these subjects.

So she had opted to try outdoor sketching before the seasons changed. Capturing the glory of the departing summer appealed to her, on many levels. The colours of the leaves and the starkness of the plants in autumn reminded her of the impermanence of all things. The sudden end of her marriage had shattered her faith in longevity. She knew it would soon be blustery and muddy.

Lena also suspected she might not be working with these students for much longer. She had not been offered a formal contract. The Hutterite doctrines did not condone divorce, so she wondered if they would ask her to leave, once her marital status, or lack of it, was publically confirmed.

Besides, Lena's husband had been behaving very strangely since he served her with the divorce petition. She had heard that he now spent an unprecedented amount of time drinking coffee with the baseball cap-wearing slugs in the local diners — men whom he had previously scorned as lazy, ignorant gossips. She could only guess which stories had filtered through to the principal. He had probably heard several juicy versions, but he probably also knew he could not grill her about them in an interview.

Lena pushed the rest of the messy implications aside and returned her focus to the children in front of her. They were still standing in a cluster on the edge of the ploughed field, awaiting further instructions. This sudden switch to docility unnerved her.

"Is that the under-land over there?" Lena asked Emily.

"Yo, it is where the cows used to live. But we do not have cows anymore. The bush is growing up. There is a river in there. Behind by the big trees. I am a bit scared now the old horse is gone. I used to come here often when she lived in there." Emily sighed at the end of her long speech.

"I didn't know you had a horse here on the colony. Do you like horses?"

"Yo, I love them. The mare was skinny and speckled, with a skeleton back, but I loved her very much. The older boys used her to chase the cows in the pasture."

"Okay, we're almost there," Lena said to the boys, as they rushed through the sagging gap in the barbed wire fence. "Pick a spot in the pasture and find something to look at. I expect you to sit and draw for the rest of the class. Please stay where I can see you. We've done enough running for today."

As soon as the words came out of her mouth, the curly-headed Jeremiah, bounding along in front of her on the barely discernible cow-path, disappeared. He squeaked three times, before she could get to the location of his last sighting.

Jeremiah had fallen into a large crevice, overgrown with burrs and thistles, created by spring runoff heading toward the river. Lena knelt on its edge, reached down and pulled the squirming boy up to level ground. His wiry body shook as she lifted him. She could not tell if his wiggles were from laughing or crying.

He was now even dirtier than after the skunk-chasing, with several burrs embedded in his hair. Prairie gumbo covered patches of his face, arms, and clothes. After he righted himself, he wiped his pants with his hand and then smeared his cheeks with them. He straightened his shoulders, pausing to readjust his black suspenders with splayed fingers. Lena attempted to pat dirt from his soiled shirt and wondered about the laundry duties of his mother. This thought was instantly diverted. The six other students broke into another chorus of hoots as Jeremiah began to comb out the burrs with his fingers.

"Ouch! Ouch!" Jeremiah hollered, in apparent agony. These shrill whoops intensified the hilarity.

Jeremiah continued to shout in pain, but Lena noticed his eyes twinkled as he yelled. She realized this noisy performance was now being played out for comic effect. Each time Jeremiah rooted in his tangled curls, he tugged the stubborn burr loose and flung it at Abraham. Abraham pitched them back. It was as if a gun had been fired to signal the start of another game. Immediately, all six boys shoved each other toward the gaping hole. They yelped a collective war cry, tore burrs off nearby stalks, and tossed the barbed seeds at each other. Franklin stretched one suspender away from his shoulder, lodged a burr in the black fabric between his thumbs, and twanged it like a slingshot to fire the small missile at Hansel's face. He repeated this attack several times. Then the rest of the boys began to shoot burrs with their suspenders.

Emily stood on the edge of the bank with her arms folded, clucking at their antics. She watched her new teacher's every move. Lena knew Emily expected her to end this latest bout of foolishness.

But Lena was still recovering from the skunk encounter and the disappearance of a student down a hole. She did not react for about thirty seconds. Then she shoved back her shoulders and straightened her spine. *"Stop right now! Stop throwing those things at each other!"*

To her surprise, they listened. They stopped chucking burrs, jerked their heads up and cocked their ears. Then they looked down at the crumbling mud. Lena stood only five foot seven in her sock feet, but at the moment, she felt as if she had sprouted up, so that she now towered over these young Hutterites.

She hated shouting at students. To her, it meant a sign of stress and failed classroom management. She knew she was under great emotional pressure. Getting them back under control would require utmost concentration. Sharply, but quietly, she commanded, "Sit down! Right here. Put your clipboards in your laps. Pick something to draw. A tree. A plant. A fence post. Anything. And start drawing. If you finish one thing, you can do another. You have lots of sheets. I want you to keep drawing for the rest of the class."

In unison, they looked up at her. Then they turned to Franklin. He slid his suspender back into its proper place and smirked. Then he nodded and muttered something in German. The rest dropped their ammunition.

Once they were perched in a row on the edge of the crevasse, she breathed slowly in and out several times. The children placed clipboards on their knees and peered across the gap. Lena noticed that each piece of paper, except for Emily's, was smeared with streaks of dirt. For five minutes, she stood over them while they stared at the opposite bank and made marks on their papers. When it appeared as if they were going to sit still for a few minutes, she plunked down beside Jeremiah with her clipboard and began to draw.

Lena's concentration grew; she became more aware of her surroundings. The autumn sun shone down through the yellowing oak leaves and the ever-present smell of burning stubble hung in the air. She took a long, deep breath. The dried-up creek bed gave off a pungent smell, a combination of rotting leaves and exposed earth. Through her track pants, on her buttocks, she felt the cool dampness of the clay. Lena gazed up at the scudding clouds and decided that after so many bouts of laughter and laps around the tilled field, the children were now tired enough to pay attention. The cool northern breeze could not touch them, nestled here amongst the sheltered quiet of the under-land. In this overgrown, abandoned pasture, an unexpected mood of serenity had descended. It surprised her, after the mayhem of the burr wars. When she had relaxed enough to think clearly, she realized she was drawing a cartoon of Jeremiah in profile, with blotchy streaks on his cheeks and large, prickly seeds poking out from his curls.

Jeremiah ducked his head and giggled when she revealed her sketch to him. Then he untangled a burr from his hair and gently placed it on the top of her head. She laughed as she disengaged it from her own strands. He tipped his muddy clipboard so she could see his drawing.

"I see a big black spot." Lena gently tapped his paper, pointing to a dark smudge on the page, surrounded by squiggles. "And here are some curly lines."

"Yo, that is where you saved me from. Those are prickers beside it. You can see my face in the hole. I am not in it any more, but I wanted to draw me."

When Lena examined the dark spot more closely, she saw a small, smiling face, carefully rendered, tucked in amongst the smudges and the squiggles. Her hand reached up to tousle Jeremiah's curls. He winked at her.

At three-fifteen, when the children trooped back to the classroom so they could be assigned their daily roster of cleaning chores, she noticed they gave the skunk carcass a wide berth. She also noticed, as they walked, they showed each other their nature drawings from the under-land.

It was the end of her first afternoon class with them. Even though she had supervised only one especially long art lesson, and only seven students, she was exhausted. Her intuition was right. It was going to very different working here at the Pine Grove colony. If she was invited back. If she wanted to come back.

# The English Cousin

KRISTA DROVE HER PADDLE, HARD, INTO THE WATER.

She closed her eyes for the length of the stroke, but glints of sunlight still burned through her eyelids. Even though she wore only a swimsuit, blue jean cut-offs, and a life jacket, the August heat had raised a coat of sweat on her skin. She inhaled and opened her eyes. Everything in the canoe smelled of wood smoke and swamp water.

For two days, the teenage girls had paddled down the chain of seven lakes, linked by the meandering Kettle River. On the first day and a half, the river's flow had pulled them along, in its steadfast and silent grip, intent on reaching Lake Winnipeg. Now they were headed home, moving at a slower pace. Where the river narrowed, they had to lean forward and exert the full force of shoulders and arms and torso to make any headway against the current.

The weather had stayed warm and calm, no rain, not a stray cloud. Night temperatures hovered above 18 degrees. No mosquitoes. After twilight, a squashed orange moon hung low in the sky. Every evening, Krista convinced her two companions to join her for moonlit swims, stroking nude and strong up the ribbon of wavering reflections.

Rock Lake stretched away from the canoe's gunwales, a couple of kilometres in each direction. Its surface was almost flat, a sky-blue sheet — rippled, like a silky fabric laid in haste. From her seat at the stern, she looked across green and yellow nylon packs, and canvas sacks puffed up with sleeping bags.

Canned food, pots, pans, and utensils nestled in a wooden crate.

Krista could not imagine any situation as close to perfect as this summer afternoon. Intoxicated by sun and open water, she felt a bubble of joy rise in her chest. She smiled at her canoe mates, but they did not notice. They had their backs to her.

Closest to her bent knees sat her cousin, Emily.

She was visiting Krista's family for the month of August. At the end of the summer, Emily was scheduled to fly home for her final year of high school in Sussex, England, and Krista and her friend Maggie were scheduled to move into Winnipeg to start university.

Emily sat on the bottom, wedged in between the rear and middle thwarts, on a blue foam pad. If Krista wanted, she could lean forward and mess up Emily's short hair. Her cousin refused to wear headgear. Krista tugged her ball cap lower on her forehead. *Only mad dogs and English maids go out in the midday Manitoba sun. Without a frickin' hat.*

Maggie, dark-haired and dark-eyed, sat in the bow, wearing a battered gray Stetson. She had moved away three years ago, not long after Krista's mother died. In a strange coincidence, Maggie's father had died a year before Krista's mother. Both deaths were from cancer.

After the loss of her husband, Maggie's mother got sick, from heart problems and stress, trying to run the family resort on her own. She sold it the next spring and moved her family to the city. But Maggie returned every summer to work at Jackie's Bake Shop, in the small community of Lost Lake. Krista also worked in Lost Lake, in the campground, cleaning toilets and picking up litter. They saw each other almost every day.

Because of the heat and lack of wind, the two girls in front of Krista dipped their blades at uneven intervals. They didn't need to exert themselves. They had the rest of the afternoon to paddle back to their launch site.

Krista shifted on her seat. Although she knew this luminous afternoon had to end, the ache of happiness had lodged deep under her sternum. She opened her mouth. "*The hiiills are aliiiive with the sound of musiiiic.*" She took a deep breath. "*I go to the hills when my heart is. . . .*"

Maggie leered over her shoulder and yelled, "Horny!"

Emily held her paddle in both hands, banged it on the thwart and chanted. "Humpin' mad! Need shaggin' bad!"

Krista lifted her own wooden blade and flicked a slice of water at her cousin's head.

Emily ran her hands through her wet hair. "Cheers. Thanks for the splash. I was bloody hot."

Krista cleared her throat. She sang, "*I go to the bush when my heart is. . . .*"

"Horny!" Maggie shouted again. She lifted her paddle in mid-stroke, laid it across her lap and turned her head. "Tell Emily about hunky Gil and how he goes to your bush."

Krista stopped singing. "Okay. In July, I did *it* with Gilbert, the rich boy with the big cottage across Eagle Bay. We were drunk and he hit his head on the upper bunk."

"Where?"

"At that little cabin we built. On McCoy Lake."

"How Canadian! Losing one's virginity in a log cabin." Emily hooted.

Krista closed her eyes and mumbled, "Well, I wasn't. Not exactly . . . a virgin."

Her cousin hadn't heard. She was still laughing.

Then Emily turned as far around as she could, careful not to unbalance the narrow craft, and sang, "*Tell me more! Tell me more!*"

Maggie yelped and covered her ears. "Are you two trying to make me puke? First Julie Andrews and now Olivia Newton John. Have you *ever* been mellow?"

Krista ignored them and continued to sing every lyric she could remember from the *The Sound of Music*.

Twenty minutes later, they paddled into a narrower section of the Kettle River. Krista shifted on her seat, thrust her paddle into the water and pulled hard. "Sorry, folks, performance is over. We have to give 'er!"

"Aye, captain." Despite her awkward position and shorter arms, Emily reached over the gunwales to make sweeping strokes. The next lake was about one kilometre away.

Krista watched Emily as they rounded the bend in the river. It unsettled, but gladdened, her to observe her cousin. No one in the world, not even her sister Ingrid, resembled Krista so much. She and Emily had similar green eyes and a direct gaze. Also, Emily's hair was a few shades darker, and her skin was porcelain pale. She stood a full head shorter and was left-handed, like Krista's mother. But Emily laughed like Krista, loud and outright. She loved horses and the outdoors, and showed a great willingness for adventure. When asked about a canoe trip, she had replied, without hesitation, "Brilliant, I'd love to go."

ON THE FIRST OF AUGUST, during the two-hour ride home from the airport, Krista had recognized she'd met her doppelganger. Their caustic jokes fit together like gears on a watch. Back in Lost Lake, they kept Maggie laughing for hours, with proclamations on English superiority versus Canadian, and wisecracks about sex. This amazed Krista. Was humour genetic?

It also troubled her to watch her cousin. She could see that Emily possessed a natural and energetic beauty. If Krista looked like her, did this mean she was attractive, too? The idea terrified her.

"A motorboat's coming around the big boulder!" Maggie yelled. "We need to pull over to the edge of the channel."

Krista swung her J-stroke hard to the left, banging it against the rear hull.

Moving at half-speed, a sixteen-foot aluminum boat with a small Evinrude motor approached.

Maggie said, "The guy steering looks like Dean Russell. That park police asshole. He's with a bulky older guy. Maybe Dean wants to catch some fish poachers. Hey, Krista, do you have a license?"

Yesterday, they had caught and eaten a couple of jackfish. Krista tucked her dismantled rod under the edge of the foam pad that Emily used for a seat. "I thought you had one."

Maggie laughed. "Speaking of hardened criminals, did you tell Emily how Dean caught us skinny-dipping at Gibson Beach that hot night in July?"

"Nope."

"So I'll tell the story. He was on patrol in the Lost Lake campground and decided to check if anyone was breaking the eleven o'clock beach curfew. We saw his truck drive up so we swam out further. Krista was super worried she might get fired for breaking campground rules. For fifteen minutes, Dean flared his big club of a flashlight across the water and yelled. When we wouldn't come out, he confiscated our clothes. Then we crawled over a pile of rocks, up a cliff, and through a patch of wild roses to get back to my camper trailer. Mosquitoes chewed the hell out of our bare asses."

Emily laughed and nodded. Despite the scarcity of bugs this late in the summer, her pale ankles were spotted and swollen. "Is Dean hunting you down to return your knickers?"

"I doubt it." Maggie pointed at the approaching boat. "He's got his binoculars out. Damn pervert is spying on us."

Krista said, "Do you remember a tall guy with bushy red hair and freckles, when we registered our trip at the campground office? Dressed like Smoky the Bear?"

Emily didn't answer but held her left hand above the line of her eyebrows and peered at the boat, then shifted to avoid the end of the fishing rod poking her butt cheek.

"Dean's got a reputation. He'll screw anyone," Maggie said.

She heard a lot of gossip in the bakery. The park police guys often came in for coffee and doughnuts after their first patrol.

"Oh shit. The old guy — in the baseball cap — it's your father, Krista."

They stopped paddling. The current caught the canoe. It slid backwards.

"What the. . . ." The sight of her father wrenched Krista's euphoria away, like someone yanking a cloth off a table. She stared at the boat. The sweat on her upper body chilled. She unbuckled her life jacket and pulled a tee-shirt over her shoulders.

Maggie gave a few strokes, pushing her blade deep into the water, but they didn't have much effect, since she was the only one paddling and the current on this corner was relentless. "Why would he hang out with Dean Russell? He hates conservation guys. Every deer season, they try to catch him without a tag."

Krista put her life jacket back on. "Yeah, he cuts them off and reuses them."

Emily shifted again. "Did you tell your parents when we'd be back?"

"I told Victoria, my beloved stepmother," Krista said.

She picked up her paddle, but did not take a stroke. *What's that bastard doing here? He's never come looking for Maggie and me. And we've been up and down this river dozens of times. Even on that day when we battled gale-force winds and buckets of rain, he only bitched about the possibility of the canoe getting wrecked.*

Dean stalled the Evinrude when he got closer and let the boat drift. He turned the motor like a rudder, intending to come alongside the canoe, bow to bow. Dean smiled at them and waved. Krista's father pulled his dirty cap lower over his eyes and tilted forward. They could only see the bottom half of his face.

"Hey, girls, how are you doin'?" Dean hollered.

"Fine, until you showed up." Maggie reached downed for her canteen, took a swig, and glared. She pulled out a bag of sunflower seeds and shoved a handful into her cheek.

The motorboat came at them faster than Dean expected. It was obvious that he hadn't accounted for the current.

Maggie spat out a few shells. "Hey, Mr. Park Police, you'd look pretty stupid if you smashed into our canoe and capsized us."

Once he realized she wasn't going to grab the boat's bow, he turned and yanked the starter cord. The Evinrude coughed and chugged, then caught. He slammed into reverse, a half metre from the canoe.

Krista lowered her paddle in the water. It was difficult to manoeuvre a canoe when it was travelling backward, but not impossible. Her father raised the front of his ball cap and smiled at Emily. He said something, but the words got lost in the sudden roar of the outboard. Maggie cupped her hand to her ear and shrugged.

Emily looked back at Krista, and then turned to watch her uncle. He yelled at Dean, "For fuck's sake, didn't your boss teach you how to drive a boat?"

Dean twisted the throttle the wrong way and the motor revved louder.

Krista's father shouted again, but only Maggie heard. She said, "He wants Emily to know her dear Uncle Henry has come to rescue us."

Dean switched to low gear and straightened the motorboat. He trolled, parallel to the backward movement of the canoe, fighting to control the boat's momentum. At intervals, he jerked into reverse to maintain its position in the current. He kept it close, but not too close.

Krista watched Dean struggle. His face flushed pink from his exertions. *He can see we don't need rescuing. His boss will be pissed when he finds out he's wasted time and a full tank of gas on a fake emergency.*

Krista's father yelled again.

"He said we should grab hold of their rope. They'll tow us."

Maggie relayed the message over her shoulder.

Krista said, "Tell him to go fuck himself."

Maggie put her hands around her mouth and shouted at the men. "No thanks. I don't have to be at work until after five."

Then she smiled at Dean and yelled, "Do you have my underpants?"

Dean cut the engine again. "Hey, we can get you home in no time."

Krista spoke, low but forceful. "Go arrest someone starting a forest fire. Or skinny dipping."

Dean glanced at Krista's father, as if awaiting instructions. But the old man just moved around on his seat to stare at the girls. Dean rolled his eyes, turned and yanked the starter cord. This time, the engine roared to life. He swung the boat in a wide circle and came alongside the canoe, then shifted into neutral. Now both boats were pointed in the same direction.

Krista thrust her blade deep and pulled back, so hard the canoe surged forward. "All right, we've fooled around long enough."

Emily and Maggie picked up their paddles and stroked, as forcefully as Krista. Dean kept his distance, to avoid making a wake, and stretched higher to check for obstructions. Krista's father kept watching the girls.

TEN MINUTES LATER, the two boats reached open water at the north end of Crocus Lake. The wind had come up on the middle of the lake, but the girls paddled, without stopping. They did not speak to each other or to the men. Dean no longer stretched tall and vigilant, but was now slumped almost as low as Krista's father.

At the south end of Crocus Lake, they approached a rock tunnel. This narrow passageway had been blasted out, over a century earlier, when the railway was built. Krista stroked faster. She wanted to reach it first. Only one boat could fit through at a time.

Near the mouth of the tunnel, Dean smacked his boat into a submerged rock. The current pushed the hull sideways across it, making a loud scraping noise. The propeller bounced up and the motor roared. Dean shoved it back into the water and shifted into reverse to get lined up again for the tight entrance. By then, the girls were halfway into the darkness and could see the light at the opposite end.

Maggie stopped paddling and tapped her blade on the rock wall. "We've escaped those idiots, but I can still hear your old man cursing Dean."

"I love these tunnels. Nothing like this in England," Emily said. "Are your parents really concerned about us?"

"Krista's stepmom doesn't give two shits about her." Maggie said.

Krista said, "He just wanted to show off."

"Pardon?" Emily said.

"He wanted to do something special for you."

They paddled on, into the eerie, dripping quiet. Krista hooted a couple of times, but the usual fun of making echoes was diluted. When they pulled out of the tunnel, Dean accelerated past them so quickly his wake almost tipped the canoe.

Maggie spat a mouthful of sunflower shells into the water. "I guess he's not going to give me my panties. He's had enough trolling for one afternoon."

The girls laughed, and then worked hard to propel the canoe forward in the tricky currents. After the damp coolness of the rock walls, the afternoon sun felt brighter and hotter. The chill began to leave Krista's body.

By THREE O'CLOCK, they had loaded the canoe and all their gear onto Maggie's Toyota pickup. Krista tightened the last knot, slapped her hands together, and grinned. "Let's grab a beer at Cedar Lodge."

Emily shrugged. "Sounds brilliant, but I'm not old enough."

"They won't ask. Lewis, the bartender, lusts after Maggie.

He knows she's turned eighteen."

"Right. Let's down a pint and get Maggie back to work."

Maggie smiled. "Jackie won't mind. On the late shift, all I do is wash pans. And serve coffee and baked products to park police slugs."

They walked up the hill to the outdoor patio of the lodge's bar.

At five o'clock, they dropped Maggie at the bakery. After they ate a couple of doughnuts, Krista drove the Toyota back to her house. They unloaded the paddles, life jackets, and camping gear beside the front porch and untied the canoe.

Krista pulled the rope through a hole in the wooden rack. "We'll carry it down to the beach. The path's steep here but it's easier than lugging it on the longer trail by the road."

She sniffed a few times. "Smells like Victoria whipped up another fine dinner."

Emily said, "She thinks all Brits adore roast beef and Yorkshire pudding."

"It's last year's heifer. I wonder if the old man told her where he was." Krista knelt to undo the last knot from the truck's rear frame.

Emily bent over, on the opposite side of the pickup, until she could see Krista's face. She whispered. "You can ask him. He's coming out of the house."

"Oh, shit."

Emily straightened up, but Krista stayed under the truck. She could see her father's steel-toed boots facing Emily's sneakers. There was a short silence.

He said, "Victoria was very worried. She asked me to check on you."

Emily took two steps backwards. "Cheers. We're home now. Not that we were in danger. Maggie and Krista are very experienced."

"But Victoria doesn't know the bush."

Under the frame, Krista sang quietly, *"He goes to the bush when his hard-on is lonely. . . ."*

Emily coughed and chuckled.

He said, "Krista, hurry up and haul that canoe down to the dock. Emily, come eat. Victoria's made a special meal."

Emily said, "I'm sure Krista could carry it down the hill. But I'll help her."

He kicked at the gravel and spat into the woodpile. "Don't be too long. It's getting cold."

From under the truck, Krista listened and watched. His boots clunked along the driveway and onto the wooden steps of the back porch.

It was the Labour Day long weekend, and Maggie was lucky enough to get off work at the bakery and Krista had already been laid off from the campground crew. To mark Emily's departure and the summer's end, the three girls decided to take a horseback trip to an abandoned farm, located near the railroad tracks, close to where they had paddled through the rock tunnels.

During the Depression, families had carved out small homesteads along the tracks. The farm they chose to visit was the biggest and its owners, the Hansons, had stayed on the land the longest. When a chimney fire destroyed their house and two children died in the flames, they gave up and moved to Easton. Three surviving Hanson kids had attended high school with Krista's older brothers, Eric and Will.

A small bunkhouse still stood, about a hundred metres from the charred foundation, and a log barn also remained intact. Though it leaned into the wind and the spine of the roof sagged in the middle, like a saddle, their horses could be left untied in the box stalls.

Every summer, Krista's family paid the Hansons and baled the hundred acres of wild grass. Although they'd completed the second cut, they hadn't picked up all the bales. This stack lay on the far side of the meadow where the hills rose away from Beaver Creek. For trips such as this one, they left a few bales in the barn's loft. Krista loved to gallop across the mowed field, waving her hat, when trains rumbled past. Engineers always hooted a shrill whistle, to let her know they saw her.

On Friday, after lunch, they packed up the horses, rearranging knapsacks and saddle bags crammed with cans of stew and beans. The bunkhouse had a table and chairs, pots, wood stove, and three double-tiered beds built of rough lumber. The old well still worked and, this time of year, crabapple and plum trees drooped with overripe fruit. They only needed their cans of food and their sleeping bags.

Victoria came out of the house and handed them a parcel of corned beef sandwiches. Emily thanked her and the girls mounted up. They touched heels to horse's sides and headed away from the barn. When they passed the machine shed, the door swung open and Krista's brother, Eric, in grease-covered overalls, came out. He sauntered over with a small rifle in his hands. The stock was not made of wood but constructed of metal rods. He approached the horses carefully and gestured for Krista to dismount. She swung down from her bay mare, Juniper.

"Here, take this."

Emily was mounted on Chico, the pinto pony. She leaned toward Eric. "What kind of gun is that? It looks right flimsy."

"It's a .22. Will bought it off some old trapper. It can be broken in two pieces." Eric unscrewed the barrel from the stock and handed it to Krista.

Krista took the gun and examined it. "Why are you giving it to me?"

"Last week, Blake and I drove out to Hanson's farm. He's growing weed in the old garden. We saw a mother bear and two cubs eating the plums and apples. Use it to scare them. Here are some cartridges."

Krista shoved the box of bullets in her vest pocket, untied her sleeping bag, rolled the dismantled rifle into it, and tied it against the cantle of her saddle. She had to swing her leg higher to remount.

Maggie sat on Rocket, the tall dun gelding. He pawed at the gravel, anxious to get moving. Rocket was skittish, but he'd tire quicker than the other horses and Maggie could soon relax. They set off, riding single file along the narrow shoulder of highway 25. The farm lay twelve kilometres off the pavement, at the end of a rough gravel trail. Tourist traffic was sparse on the highway, but would build later in the afternoon. By then, they'd be on the bush road. This rough track crossed over Beaver Creek, where the culvert had been partially washed out.

They reached the turn-off by three o'clock and the Hanson farm by four. Krista wanted to gallop full tilt across the open field, but the horses were tired, especially Rocket, who slouched along with his tail tucked between his hind quarters and his head down. They led the horses into the barn, unsaddled and brushed them.

Maggie fetched two pails of water from the well and Krista led Emily up the rickety ladder into the upper level, where they could throw down a couple of bales. The loft door had long ago fallen off. They looked out the opening, across the expanse of cut grass. The sweet smell of dried hay hung in the confined air. A light breeze blew from the south. For Krista, it felt like a person blowing on her face — warm and moist and intimate, just strong enough to cool her sun-warmed cheeks.

Emily gazed at the forest. "What scenery. Wild and uninhabited, yet here's a lovely farm in the middle of nowhere. I hate to go back to England."

"I'm happy you came. And I'm glad you like this place."

"It's been good." She ran her left hand through her hair. "Except when your father tried to rescue us. I have to admit that I find him a bit creepy. I can't relax."

Krista replied in a deliberate, quiet voice. "No one can relax around him. One night last summer, I caught him in Maggie's truck. She was parked outside our house, waiting for me to shower and change out of horse clothes. He was drunk and climbed in and tried to grope her. She punched him and we both dragged him out and took off. Maggie didn't tell her mom. She thought it was somehow her fault."

"Shit."

"I didn't bother telling Victoria. She thinks the sun shines out of his ass."

"How do you stand it? I'd be mortified if my dad tried something like that."

"I hate it. I avoid inviting friends to my house. If they come over, I watch him all the time. I was so worried when I found out you'd be coming to visit."

Emily touched her cousin on the arm. Krista clenched her jaw and laid her palm on top of Emily's hand. *It's almost dark. I hope she can't see my eyes. I hate crying.*

Emily said, "He hasn't tried anything funny with me."

Krista exhaled. "Good. And we're all leaving in a few days."

They heard the clanking sounds of Maggie returning with pails and went down to help. The girls fed and watered the horses and carried their packs over to the bunkhouse. They propped open its wooden door, lit a fire in the tin stove, put cans of food on the shelves, and arranged their bedding and foam pads on the slats of the wooden beds.

Krista unrolled her sleeping bag. The rifle dropped out and rattled the bed frame. "Shit, I forgot about the gun."

"Bring it along. We'll go for a walk before supper," Maggie said.

Emily nodded and clapped her hands together. "Good idea. Mum would be upset if I got eaten by bears right before I started sixth form."


FOR AN HOUR, they wandered across the stubble, through overgrown gardens, amongst the fruit trees. They found Blake's cultivated patch and joked about drying some leaves for a weekend supply of dope. Then they collected a few ripe plums and speckled apples in their tee-shirts and headed back to the bunkhouse.

Krista roused the fire, put on a kettle to boil, and passed around Victoria's thick sandwiches. They ate in silence and competed to see who could spit the plum pits furthest out the wide door. This late in the summer, darkness always came earlier than expected. After a couple of candle-lit card games, Krista went out to check on the horses.

The sky hung above her, pitch black, full of stars, and the barn lay quiet in the dark. She opened the door, but did not go inside. The only noise she could hear was horses munching. She inhaled their scent, comforted by its familiarity. An owl hooted, then swooped low across the nearby field and landed. A doomed vole squeaked. She stared at the sky for fifteen minutes. When she returned to the bunkhouse, Maggie and Emily were wrapped in their down bags, fast asleep, as she'd left them.

THE NEXT DAY DAWNED WARM AND DRY. They woke early, ate beans for breakfast and packed a loaf of bread, canned ham, and peaches for lunch. Krista rolled the rifle in her jacket and tied it with the leather straps behind her saddle. The horses had recovered so the girls rode deep into the forest, along a trail that connected five abandoned farms. They stopped at every yard, dismounted, and explored the collapsed buildings. Tools and rusty machines cluttered grass-clogged yards. Barbed wire fences sagged and drooped around the perimeters of tiny fields.

At the last farm, they tied the horses, sat on a downed pine tree and ate lunch.

Emily said, "They worked so hard to clear these farms. The isolation must have terrified them if they got sick or injured."

Krista stood up and kicked at a rotten fence post. It shattered from the impact.

"Yep, life's a bitch and then you die," Maggie said. She lifted the metal lid off a barrel and recoiled at the foul smell. A family of dead mice floated in the water. "Let's head back."

They mounted and trotted along the trail.

When they reached the open expanse of the Hanson fields, they saw that a flock of Canada Geese had landed near the widest part of Beaver Creek. The birds honked and flapped and hunted in the stubble for fresh shoots of grass. The girls slowed the horses to a walk and circled around behind the haystack. It had been piled on the crest of the hill, to keep it dry, out of the clay near the creek. They tied their reins through the loops of bale twine and climbed up the side of the stack. The tarpaulin crackled and crinkled under their weight, but they made it to the top layer where they lay flat on the canvas to watch the geese.

Maggie looked across at Krista. "Why did you bring that gun up here?"

"I don't know." Krista slid a bullet into the chamber. "It's much too far away."

Emily said, "Well, although I detest hunting, even I know you don't kill game birds with a little rifle. You get close and use a shot gun."

Maggie nodded. "I bet it doesn't even shoot straight. Might blow off a piece of your face."

Krista raised the metal stock to her cheek. "Yeah, you're probably right."

She squeezed the trigger. A tinny pop exploded near her ear.

Maggie pointed at the flock, now rising in loud, single sweep off the lower field. "One goose is flapping around!"

They scrambled and slid off the noisy canvas. Chico and Juniper stood calm, all four feet on the ground. Rocket twisted and reared against the pressure of his reins. Krista reached for his headstall, hoping to get close enough to his face, to calm him, but it was too late. The gelding flung himself backwards in one final lunge, snapped both reins, spun in perfect pivot and ran.

Krista yelled, "Forget that mule! He'll just run back to the barn and get into the bag of oats we brought." She unscrewed the gun's two parts, rolled it back into her jacket, and tied it. Then she mounted Juniper and gestured for Maggie to climb up behind her saddle. "We need to put that bird out of its misery."

Emily jumped onto Chico. They galloped across the field to where the goose thrashed around on the muddy banks. One wing drooped at its side. Krista flung her leg over Juniper's mane and dismounted before the horse had stopped moving. Where the bullet had pierced its lung, a patch of blood oozed onto gray-white chest feathers. By the time Maggie dismounted and scooped up Juniper's reins, Krista had twisted the goose's neck.

"Remind me not to hang around you, if I get hurt," Emily said, after she rode up on Chico and dismounted.

"I still can't believe I hit it."

Maggie patted Juniper's shoulder. "Easy, easy, girl. Look how she reacts to the smell of blood."

"Nah, she just misses her brainless barn mate."

A freight train's long whistle startled them. Krista picked up the goose carcass and held it behind the bulk of her horse.

"You do know it is several weeks until bird season? You'd better hide it." Maggie climbed onto Juniper's saddle. "I'm heading back. I think I see that bonehead standing by the barn door. You can walk to the bunkhouse. With your precious goose."

THAT NIGHT, KRISTA RIGGED UP A SPIT, using two pieces of harrow and an iron rod. They gutted and plucked the goose, and then impaled it with the rod. After they lit a large bonfire, they dragged three chairs out of the bunkhouse, sat down, and watched the goose roast. Every time they turned its carcass, they threw salt and pepper on the crackling skin.

They ate the warm, dark meat, along with slices of Victoria's homemade bread, sat around the fire, drank Southern Comfort, and watched poplar logs burn. Off in the distance, the sun settled behind the opening where the train tracks led straight into the forest. The meal had made them sleepy, but the liquor made them talkative.

Maggie took a sip and raised her finger to her lips. "I hear a truck."

"It's out on highway 25." Krista slurred more than necessary. She liked how the words slid out of her mouth, like wet candies.

"It's too loud. And we're too far in the bush," Maggie said.

"I can hear it." Emily stopped drinking and leaned back in her chair to listen.

"Could be Blake and Eric." Maggie made a sad face as she looked into her tin cup. "Maybe they'll bring more liquor."

"Blake is cute," Emily said.

"Yeah, too bad he smells. Never showers. No one knows why." Maggie slurped up the last of her drink and stood up to toss another log on the fire. "I can see the headlights now. Crossing the tracks."

"You're right. It's not on the highway." Krista stood beside Maggie and watched the truck approach. It spun and bounced, lights flickering on the wall of surrounding trees.

"Maybe it's the park rangers, come to find out who shot their favourite goose." Emily looked at the greasy bones piled in the frying pan and giggled.

Krista threw the remains into the fire. "We must destroy the evidence."

She picked up the axe as the truck swerved off the rough road and drove fast across the stubble, almost right up to the bunkhouse. It slid to a halt on the other side of a sagging pole fence. The driver got out and walked toward them.

"Looks like Will's truck," Maggie said.

Krista put down the axe and returned to her chair. The figure came closer.

Maggie kicked the end of a half-burnt log into the middle

of the flames and sat down beside her. "Ah shit, it's your father. I can't believe this. Twice in two weeks."

He strode into the circle of light. "Emily! Are they keeping you up late?"

They could not see it at first, but he staggered, or over-swaggered, as he approached. A twelve pack of Molson Canadian dangled from his right hand. None of the girls greeted him.

"I thought you might be thirsty." He grabbed a stump, stood it vertical on the ground, sat down, and set the case between his legs. With his pocketknife, he sawed off the cardboard lid and cracked open two bottles. "Here, Emily, have a nice, cold Canadian beer."

"No thanks." Emily's polite accent hung in the damp night air, an admonishment to his invasion.

"I know you're not old enough and I know you got falling-down drunk at that beach party. I don't give a shit. But Victoria was concerned your mother might think we're a bad influence." He handed one of the bottles to Emily.

She took it and placed it on the ground.

"What's wrong? Won't drink with your Uncle Henry?"

"Go home. You're pissed." Krista's slur had disappeared. Her words now came out loud and cold. The more her father spoke, the more she realized how drunk he was.

"Fuck you. I wasn't talking to you."

"Go home. Right now."

"You don't own this place. I'm trespassing. Just like you."

Maggie stood up. "We wanted a nice, private evening. Before Emily leaves."

"What kind of girls hang out in the bush? You need a man around."

"Not you. Go home." Krista stared at the axe, beside the pile of firewood.

"What are you? Bunch of fucking lesbians?"

"Go home." Her voice was louder, torn and ragged.

He stood up, faced Maggie, and waggled his beer bottle in

front of her nose. "You think you're hot shit. Well, Emily likes my style. She wants me here."

He walked over and wrapped his right arm around Emily's shoulder.

"I most certainly do not!" Emily flung the arm off her shoulder, got up, and stood beside Maggie.

"He's not interested in logic," Krista said.

Her father faced Emily, wrapped his arms around her and pulled her toward him, slamming her hard against his chest. He tried to kiss her on the mouth, but she turned her face away and he ended up slobbering on her neck.

Maggie and Krista jumped at him to pry them apart. Krista grabbed his right arm and twisted. He wrenched it away, shoved Maggie to the ground with that same arm, then punched his daughter high in the forehead, hard enough to knock her flat. She landed beside the fire. He swore and grabbed Emily again with both arms. She screamed and kicked at his shins. He started to drag her toward the bunkhouse.

Maggie jumped up. "You asshole!"

Krista gripped the frying pan in her hand. She stood up and followed him.

"I told you to go home." She swung the metal disc at the back of his head.

He dropped Emily like a bag of oats and spun around. In the glow from the fire, she saw his face. She had never seen such a surprised look. Then it disappeared. He collapsed into the stubble about three metres away from the door.

Emily got up, brushed loose hay and dirt off her jeans. Maggie and Krista came to her side and examined her. Emily's body shook. She closed her eyes, her face crumpled, and she cried. Maggie and Krista stood on each side of her and hugged her tight. Emily collapsed into their embrace. They held her, between them, until the crying slowed.

Emily rocked from side-to-side and wiped her wet face with her hands. Several times, she repeated, "I'm all right. I'm okay."

Over Emily's head, Maggie said, "What a nut case! Thinks he can grab any woman he wants. Krista, I'm so fucking glad you smacked him!"

Krista's father moaned and rolled around in the grass. They ignored him. After a few minutes, he struggled to his feet. He stumbled toward Will's truck, cursed and muttered and rubbed the back of his head. He got into the truck, started it, and stomped on the accelerator. Chunks of dirt flew up from the rear tires.

They led Emily back to her chair and she collapsed into it.

"If we're lucky, a train will hit him." Krista carried the frying pan back to the bunkhouse and then returned to the fire. She had the three sleeping bags draped over her left arm and the rifle in her right hand. "I hope he's got a bigger lump than me."

She rubbed her forehead. Then she wrapped one of the sleeping bags around Emily's shoulders, handed one to Maggie, sat in the chair closest to Emily, and arranged her own bag around her legs. She put the gun on the ground by her chair.

"I see he left his beer," Maggie said.

After she put down her sleeping bag, she stood up, cracked open two bottles and handed them to Emily and Krista. She walked over to the woodpile, grabbed a couple of big logs and threw them onto the fire. Then she picked the bottle Emily had placed on the ground and took a swig.

She said, "I don't feel like sleeping."

Sparks flew up into the night sky and a circle of light illuminated their faces. Emily had been staring at the flames. She looked up when Maggie spoke and said, "Neither do I."

Maggie started to talk, about how she missed her father and how she worried about her mother, but mostly about what an asshole Krista's father was. Emily didn't say much. Krista didn't say much. All three of them drank quickly and Maggie handed out three more.

Krista gripped the beer in her right hand and watched the road and the trees for another flash of headlights. Every few minutes she put her hand down to touch the gun. She also watched her cousin, and Maggie, to gauge the damage. She finished her beer, put the bottle on the ground, got up and stretched her arms, into the darkness.

She said, "I should have hit him much harder, years ago. The first time he came after me."

They didn't go to bed until a thin streak of dawn appeared on the forest horizon.

ON SUNDAY AFTERNOON, they cleaned the bunkhouse and packed up. The weather had turned. It was now much colder, cloudy and hazy. While the girls saddled up, the horses shifted sideways and pranced, restless, eager to return home.

"I'll ride Rocket, if you want." Krista tucked the rifle in her sleeping bag. Her knapsack felt light on her shoulders now the cans of food were gone.

"Okay, I'll switch after he settles down."

Although the cooler weather and the horses' yearning for their familiar barn made the trip home much quicker, it was dusk by the time they rode into the yard. They headed to the barn, led the horses inside, and unsaddled.

Maggie grabbed her gear and said, "I can't stay and visit. I need to go see Jackie. She wants to give me my last pay cheque. I have to catch her before she goes to bed. She starts baking at four in the morning."

Emily and Krista followed Maggie over to her truck. She threw her knapsack and sleeping bag into the box and then turned back to them. "I had fun. See you tomorrow."

Emily hugged Maggie. "Thanks for everything. I'm knackered, but I can feed and water the horses. Krista, go tell Victoria we're back."

Krista walked over to the low bungalow and thought about the scene by the bonfire. Will's truck was parked in front of the machine shed. Her father must have made it home. *Did he explain the lump on the back of his head? Did he tell Victoria where he'd been?*

She got to the door and turned the handle. It did not open. She tugged at the knob, but it still resisted. *How was this possible?* The door to the house had never been locked, in all the years she lived there. Then she noticed the note taped against the inside of the window pane.

"I've taken Robbie and gone to visit my mother. Your father is upset with you and won't tell me why. You need to find another place to live. Say goodbye to Emily. We enjoyed her visit. — Victoria"

She stared at the note for several minutes. *What was she supposed to do?* She turned from the porch and trudged back to the barn. She yanked open the wooden door and stepped inside.

She muttered, "Bad news, we need to find a place to sleep."

No one answered. She could not see anything until her eyes adjusted. She found the switch and flicked it on. The horses had finished their feed of oats, and were nosing around, licking the rubber tubs for stray kernels. She untied them, turned them out, and watched them walk, single file, into the rough pasture. Darkness had come quickly, because of the low clouds. Drops of rain, which had hung in the sky all day, started to fall.

"Great. No bed, no supper, no Victoria, and now it's raining. And where the hell is Emily?"

As if in answer to her mumbled question, she heard a noise above her head. She could not quite name it. If asked, she might have said it sounded like a whimper.

"Ah, shit."

She turned to the wooden racks where they stored the horse equipment. Her sleeping bag was no longer tied to her saddle. They had thrown their loose gear into an unused stall. The strings holding the sleeping bag together were hard to untie after the long ride in the damp. She slid a jackknife out of her pocket, sliced through them. She flipped open the bag and the rifle fell with a clunk on the cement floor.

She grabbed it, reached in her pocket, found a couple of bullets, fumbled to load the gun. The loft could only be accessed from the outside. She slipped out the door as quietly as possible and ran around to the end of the building. Someone had propped a wooden ladder against the edge of the loft opening. She almost swore but stopped herself. Then she ran back into the barn to find a flashlight in the pile of camping gear. With rifle in one hand and flashlight wedged in her back pocket, she climbed the ladder. She held her own panicked breathing for a few seconds and heard louder noises coming out of the loft — a male voice groaning and mumbling.

She scrambled over the last rung and crawled inside. Stood up and clicked on the flashlight.

"Get away from her!"

"Fuck off, you little bitch."

In the darkness, his bare ass, highlighted by the beam from the flashlight, looked as white and wet as new plaster.

"I've got a gun. It's small, but it'd really hurt, this close to your prick."

He rolled off Emily. Although the flaps of his plaid work shirt hid his penis, she could tell by the protrusion it was erect. He glared at her, but did not get up or try to hide his naked parts. He had yanked off Emily's jacket, pulled her tee-shirt over her shoulders, and torn one bra strap. He had unzipped her jeans and pulled them halfway down her thighs. The panties were still in place.

Emily turned away from him, curled into a fetal position, and made quiet, gasping sobs.

Krista waved the rifle. "Now pull up your pants and get the hell out of here."

When he stood up, the reek of whiskey stung her eyes, almost choked her. She wanted to cry, but kept the rifle pointed at the bulge in the right pocket of his wool shirt, where he stored a single can of snuff. The flashlight shone on his face. His too-familiar features looked slack, as if melted and pulled downward.

"I said get the hell out of here."

He swore again, clambered over the top rungs, and disappeared. Once he was on the ground, he yelled up at her. "You'll be sorry."

"You're the one who's going to be sorry," she murmured and then turned to Emily.

Krista waited until Emily stopped crying and then helped her collect her clothes and get dressed. She didn't want to rush, but she was scared her father might come back. They climbed down from the loft, walked up the gravel road to the cottage next door, and asked old Mrs. Campbell if they could use her phone to call Jackie.

Maggie was still there. She picked them up right away.

In another half an hour, they were seated on the wooden benches at the Lost Lake RCMP detachment. They hadn't said much on the way to the police station, but all three knew exactly what they needed to do.

Krista shifted on the oak bench and waited for Constable Rankin to call them into the inner office. She could feel sweat on her face and arm pits, dripping down her spine. The pressure on her chest kept her from taking a full breath. Something inside her had been smashed, broken, torn forever. She considered going to the bathroom to throw up, or scream, but did not want to leave the others for a minute.

They could stay in Maggie's camper trailer for the next couple of days. Or bunk at Jackie's place. Most of all, she would miss Robbie, her youngest brother. And the horses.

Finally, she could tell someone.

She had waited for this night a long time.

CONNIE BART-HAMEL

Donna Besel grew up in Whiteshell Provincial Park, Manitoba, where she learned to love the boreal forest. She now lives on the mighty Winnipeg River and leads creative writing workshops for all ages, in many interesting places. When asked what her writing is about, she says, "Life and death."